He lower her unique fragrance. She'd noticed that he liked doing that, as though the smell of her skin gave him sensual pleasure. It turned her on, too.

Her body immediately reacted to his: her nipples grew hard and she became moist between her legs. It was a heady, all too erotic sensation that was so delicious she let out a soft sigh. She looked at his lips. He was smiling and his white teeth, coupled with those juicy lips, looked so inviting that she threw her arms around his neck and kissed him. Erik didn't need any further provocation. Her lips were soft and her mouth so sweet that before he knew it he had lifted her body and her legs were wrapped around him in a bid to get even closer. Their tongues danced gently at first and found the encounter so pleasing that the kiss deepened and soon they were both sounding as though they were consuming something extremely tasty as, no doubt, they were. Erik, as the one who had most of the physical strength between them, knew that he had to back off before things got out of hand. Ana wasn't ready for things to go any further than a kiss, but it was their first real kiss and, heaven help him, if her kisses were this good, what would sex with her be like?

It was Ana who came up for air first and looked him in the eyes. She pressed her cheek to his. "Oh, God, why haven't you kissed me before now?"

"I've been a fool," Erik said, and kissed her again.

Books by Janice Sims

Harlequin Kimani Romance

Temptation's Song
Temptation's Kiss
Dance of Temptation
A Little Holiday Temptation

JANICE SIMS

is the author of nineteen novels and has had stories included in nine anthologies. She is the recipient of an Emma Award for her novel *Desert Heat* and two Romance in Color awards: an Award of Excellence for her novel *For Keeps* and a Best Novella award for her short story "The Keys to My Heart" in the anthology *A Very Special Love*. She has been nominated for a Career Achievement Award by *RT Book Reviews,* and her novel *Temptation's Song* was nominated for Best Kimani Romance Series in 2010 by *RT Book Reviews.* She lives in Florida with her family.

A Little
HOLIDAY
Temptation

JANICE SIMS

HARLEQUIN®
entertain, enrich, inspire™

Recycling programs
for this product may
not exist in your area.

ISBN-13: 978-0-373-86286-3

A LITTLE HOLIDAY TEMPTATION

Copyright © 2012 by Janice Sims

For questions and comments about the quality of this book, please contact us at CustomerService@Harlequin.com.

www.Harlequin.com

Printed in U.S.A.

Dear Reader,

If you've read the previous Temptation books—
Temptation's Song, Temptation's Kiss and *Dance of
Temptation*—you're already familiar with Erik Whitaker
and Ana Corelli, who have been friends only for the past
two years. It was my plan to end the Temptation series
with *Dance of Temptation;* however, I received so many
messages from readers via email, JaniceSims.com and
Facebook wanting to know if Erik and Ana were going
to get their story told that I knew I had to write it.

So this book is for you!

Janice Sims

Thanks to Glenda Howard for agreeing to publish this book when I asked her if it could be my next Kimani Romance book due to heightened reader interest. Also to Shannon Criss, whose editorial assistance was most appreciated. And, as always, thanks to my agent, Sha-Shana Crichton, for her kindness and encouragement.

Chapter 1

The cab pulled up to the midtown Manhattan restaurant whose large picture windows spilled forth a welcoming golden light. After paying the driver, Ana Corelli paused a moment with her hand on the door's handle. Nervousness caused her stomach muscles to clench painfully. Today she had made a decision that would change her life forever. If anyone would understand why she'd done it, Erik would.

With a determined grimace she opened the cab's door and stepped out. She shivered a little in the cold October night's air. "Thank you."

"My pleasure, Ms. Corelli," said the driver, craning his neck to smile at her.

Ana was no longer surprised when someone recognized her. Due to magazine covers, print ads, fashion shows and TV ads, her image was all over the world. She returned his smile. "You have a good evening," she said in parting, her Italian accent slight but present. She had grown up speaking both English and Italian. Her mother was an African-American opera singer who had married an Italian and moved to Milan. Ana, her brother, Dominic, and sister, Sophia, had been taught to revere both cultures.

After the cab sped away, she smoothed her leather jacket over her skirt and adjusted the bag on her shoulder before resolutely walking toward the restaurant's entrance. The hostess, an attractive African-American woman, smiled warmly as she approached her. "Good to see you again, Ms. Corelli, Mr. Whitaker is at the bar. We anticipate a twenty-minute wait for a table."

"Thank you," said Ana pleasantly. "I'll join Mr. Whitaker at the bar, then."

"Enjoy your evening," said the hostess, and returned to her post in time to greet a young couple entering the restaurant.

Ana stopped in her tracks when she spotted Erik sitting on a barstool at the cherrywood bar, a glass of lager sitting in front of him that looked like it hadn't been touched. She smiled. He wasn't a big drinker. Today, he was wearing a tailored dark blue suit with a white shirt and maroon-striped silk tie. It was Friday and he'd probably come straight here from the office. He rarely got out of there before seven.

She slid onto the stool beside him. He looked at her reflection in the mirror behind the bar, and smiled at her. Turning to her, his eyes swept over her face. "So, how does it feel to be back in the world of the living?"

She grinned, and leaned in to kiss his cheek. He smelled good, as if he'd taken the time to shave his five-o'clock shadow in his office bathroom before leaving to meet her. She placed her hand along his strong jaw. Erik looked at her in his enigmatic way. Those golden-hued eyes seemed to bore into her soul. "I finished the last painting only a few hours ago," she told him softly. "I slept for a couple hours then woke up, phoned you, and here I am. I've missed you."

"I've missed you, too," he murmured close to her ear. The sound of his voice, as always, made her warm inside.

She'd spent the last two weeks exiled in her Greenwich Village loft, completing paintings that would comprise her first show at a New York City gallery. Erik knew this. However he didn't know why she had asked to see him tonight.

She was about to blurt it out when a woman sat down on the other side of Erik and accidentally knocked her martini glass over, causing the drink to spill onto Erik's leg. Luckily, the woman had nearly finished the drink before sitting down so Erik only received a small stain on his pants' leg.

The woman grabbed a handful of napkins from the bar's top and began pressing the wadded up napkins on top of Erik's leg, apologizing all the while. "I'm so sorry," she said, screwing up her beautiful face in a pretty pout. "I'm such a klutz."

Erik laughed shortly, and held the woman's hand at bay. If she ran her hand any higher up on his leg, she would get entirely too personal for his comfort. "It's all right," he assured her. "It's an old suit."

The woman, who was dressed in designer clothes herself, obviously knew quality when she saw it. She was certainly looking at it. He was around six-one and in great shape. His clean-shaven, square-chinned face was handsome in a rugged, utterly masculine way. His eyes were so beautiful, she could drown in them, and if his voice were any sexier, she'd melt. She peered at his shoes, his watch, how perfectly his suit fit him, his skin, his teeth, his haircut, and realized that with him, money was no object. She wouldn't have conveniently spilled her drink on him if he had looked penniless.

"At least let me buy you a drink," she said. Her big brown eyes were very persuasive.

"That's sweet of you," said Erik, "but I already have a drink, and was just about to order one for my date." He indicated Ana with a nod in her direction.

The woman looked over at Ana who had watched the scene with an amused expression. She'd seen women use that "spilled drink" trick on more than one occasion. Erik was too much of a gentleman, however, to call the woman out on it.

"Oh," said the woman, her ample chest heaving with a sigh, "I see." Still not willing to give up entirely, she withdrew a card from her purse and placed it in Erik's palm. "Perhaps we can have that drink some other time," she said for his ears only.

She smoothly removed herself from the barstool, not giving him a chance to return her card, if he was of that mind. Looking at Ana, she said in parting, "Did anyone ever tell you you're a dead ringer for Ana Corelli?"

What nerve! Ana thought angrily. She sent mental daggers into the woman's retreating back. How desperate do you have to be to boldly accost a man who was obviously with another woman? She had to take several deep breaths before she trusted herself to return her attention to Erik who was watching her with a smile touching the corners of his generous mouth. "Where were we?" he asked, coaxing her back into their intimate circle.

For a moment, Ana couldn't form words. Heat flared in her face. Now she knew how being hot under the collar felt. For some reason that woman's behavior made her fiercely protective of Erik and ready to defend her territory. But Erik wasn't her territory. They were friends. In the beginning, he had told her he was attracted to her and wanted to date her, but at that time she had just gotten out of a disastrous relationship with an egotistical actor whose treatment of her had left her insecure. She'd told Erik that they could be friends, but she was giving up on dating for a while, but she hadn't dated anyone else since they had started hanging out together. Come to think of it, neither had he that she knew of. Could he have a secret lover? Someone he hooked up with on occasion to satisfy his needs? He was a red-blooded male, after all. She had longings herself. It only stood to reason that he did, too.

Suddenly she was wondering if she were standing in his way of a real relationship. Someone he could get serious about, and consider marrying. Erik, married and no longer a major part of her life? The thought made her cringe inwardly. She could not imagine life without Erik.

"Ana?"

Ana realized Erik was waiting on her to tell him why she'd called. She cleared her throat. "I quit my day job," she announced.

Erik didn't look surprised. "You've been talking about it for a long time. Modeling doesn't make you happy, painting does. You should follow your heart."

"I still have to fulfill my cosmetics contract, plus my family's company is starting a new line of clothing for full-figured women. I'll be appearing in ads for it since I've put on a few pounds." She looked at him out of the corner of her eye to see if he'd respond to the mention of extra pounds. But there was no reaction whatsoever.

Erik only smiled. He had noticed. The added ten pounds or so made her look healthier and less angular. She'd filled out in all the right places, fuller breasts and hips, a rounder, less concave belly. He loved her new body. She had always been sexy to him. Now even sexier. He could tell she knew it, too. There was more jiggle in her walk, as if she were indeed feeling confident about her new body.

Of course, he couldn't say that out loud. They were supposed to be just friends. If she knew he coveted her body, often dreamed of making love to her, there was no telling how she would react. He remembered when he'd tried to date her in the beginning. She'd told him she'd given up on men. If he wanted to be a part of her life, he would have to be satisfied with her friendship, nothing else. It had been two long years. His frustration was coming to a head. He wanted, no, he *needed* more. Every time he resolved to tell her how he felt, however, he would talk himself out of it because having her in his life was preferable to not having her in his life at all. If she gave him any indication of feeling about him the way he felt about her, though, he would jump on the opportunity with both feet. All he needed was a sign.

The way she was looking at that woman who had come on to him could possibly be that sign. Could it be that she was possessive of him? The thought was intriguing.

The bartender took her drink order and once they were alone again, Ana regarded him with a contemplative expression on her face and said, "You and I have always been honest with each other, haven't we?"

A cautious man, Erik took a moment to wonder why she would ask that. "I've always thought so," he replied hesitantly.

Ana smiled warmly. Dimples appeared in both cheeks. Her deep brown eyes held his gaze. "Am I standing in the way of your future happiness?"

"What?" He looked genuinely puzzled. Then, he laughed. Looking down at the card lying on the bar the woman from earlier had given him, he said, "You mean that?" He met her gaze once more. "You know how I feel about you. I'm the man who's willing to wait, remember?" She detected no bitterness in his voice, which made her feel even worse.

She could let it drop but she had to get to the heart of the matter. "You don't feel as if I've been using you these past two years? I know you said you would wait until I was ready for a relationship. But maybe you've changed your mind and our being friends all this time has made you see me in a different light—as a friend. Not a lover."

Erik's brows raised in an incredulous expression. If anything, the time they'd spent together had made him fall for her even harder. They had met in Milan, on the opening night of *Temptation,* Ana's brother Dominic's modern opera, nearly two years ago. Initially, he had to admit, his attraction to her was physical. There was no denying she was gorgeous. Five ten and built for sin. Skin the color of toasted almonds. She had a heart-shaped face with big brown eyes, a well-shaped nose, full, sensually curved lips and a cleft in her chin, which gave her a distinctive look. Her naturally wavy black hair was long and usually falling down her back. Yes, all the physical parts fit together very nicely. But that was only part of why he loved Ana. To know her was to love her, and knowing her made him privy to her inner workings. For example, there was a great mind behind that beautiful face. She would rather be curled up with a good book than go to a social event where she would be the center of attention. Material posses- sions, though she could very well afford the best, were not of utmost importance to her. She gave generously of her time and money. And family meant more to her than anything else in the world.

"If you're asking if I'm no longer interested in you… romantically, then the answer is don't be ridiculous. Just give me the word and I'll throw you over my shoulder and take you to my place right now and make love to you all night long." His sensual perusal made her blush.

She demurely lowered her eyes and gave a contented sigh. So, he still wanted her. That was good to know. Now, what was she going to do about it? She raised her eyes to his. "Have you ever considered the idea of our being friends with benefits?"

Because she most certainly had—many, many times!

The bartender walked up and placed her chilled white wine in front of her, then promptly departed. She took a fortifying sip as she awaited Erik's answer. What was wrong with her tonight, she wondered. Was the fact that she had made one big decision psychologically urging her to make an even bigger one? She had been dragging her feet about their relationship because she was so content with Erik in her life. Why mess with perfection? Her last relationship had ended after she'd become intimate with the guy. It was as if getting her into bed was the ultimate goal and once that was accomplished she wasn't desirable to him anymore. And the guy before him had dropped her because she'd wanted to wait until she knew him better before going to bed with him. He had been conceited enough to tell her a requirement to being with him was sex, and lots of it. He'd called *her* a freak of nature! She was sure she was probably complicating her problem with men too much. She'd simply made bad choices in men. She was twenty-five and had had only one lover, and he'd turned out to be a bastard. Intellectually, she knew this. However, telling that to her broken heart was another thing, entirely.

Erik was so different from the others. He was solid and reliable. A brilliant businessman, he had taken his family's company to new heights. Of course, his father, John Whitaker, had given him a wonderful foundation to build upon but Erik was continuing the tradition of making the family name an honorable one in big business. Known for buying failing companies and turning them around, thereby saving the jobs of many Americans, Erik found satisfaction in a job well done.

His cognac-colored eyes held an amused expression when he answered her question, his tone seductive, "About twice a day, maybe four times a day on weekends."

Ana fanned her face. She'd flushed upon hearing him admit that. So, she wasn't the only one who had sex on the brain. "I've thought of it just as often," she admitted.

"But I'd never actually do it," said Erik, his expression turning serious. He sighed and sat up straighter on the barstool. Looking deep into her eyes, he said, "Ana, being friends with benefits means that you will somehow be able to detach yourself from your feelings while you're making love. I could never do that with you. When we make love it's going to be seriously emotional. I'm not going to hold anything back. Everything

I've wanted to express to you in a physical way over the last two years will be in every touch. So, if you want me, you'll have to take all of me, not just a part of me."

Ana was trying to calm her racing heart. The man was hot as hell. What would happen if she just let go and told him, "yes, let's go back to your place right now? It's time." Actually it was way past time to do something about the sexual tension building between them.

She was glad when the hostess approached and said their table was ready. Erik handed the bartender a tip and with it, the woman's card. "Would you mind disposing of that for me?"

He then escorted Ana to their table and helped her into her chair.

"Your waiter will be with you shortly," said the hostess, and left.

"You were saying?" Erik said, looking at Ana expectantly.

"You're right," Ana said a bit breathlessly. "We're well past the friends-with-benefits stage. I couldn't make love to you, and then return to being just friends the next day. I'm not made that way."

Erik grasped her hand. "I have to say I'm a little surprised by the suggestion. What brought this on?"

Suddenly Ana knew exactly why she hadn't given in to Erik until now. It wasn't just that she was afraid of messing up a good thing. The epiphany was a relief to her. But it also made her a little sad. Looking him straight in the eyes, Ana said, her voice awe filled, "I kept putting you off because…I didn't feel worthy of you."

"How could you have felt that way?" Erik asked. Surprise was evident in his tone.

Ana cut him off with, "I know it never crossed your mind. But listen, please. I grew up in a family of over-achievers. My mother was a world-renowned singer. My father has run the family business for decades with great success, and my sister is following in his foot-steps. Do I need to mention how beloved my brother, the maestro, is?" She paused to breathe. "Growing up, I didn't know what to do with myself. I loved to draw but in a country like Italy where so many of the great artists were born I felt more than a little intimidated. I hid my work for years, not wanting anyone to see what I'd created. Then, when I was a teenager and I just kept growing, five-ten at fifteen, someone told me I should be a model and I thought to myself, 'That's something I could be good at,' and to my utter surprise I was signed to an agency right away. But I never felt as if it were an accomplishment. After all, beauty is something you inherit from your parents. It's not something you earn."

"I think a lot of people who work hard on their physical appearance would disagree with you," Erik pointed out.

"Yes, of course I have to eat right and exercise, but this face was a gift from God," Ana countered.

"Are you feeling guilty again because your image is used to make women feel insecure?" he asked softly. "So insecure that they'll buy the products your face helps to sell in order to aim for an impossibly high standard of beauty?"

"No, it isn't, Dr. Freud. It's about leaving behind something lasting when I'm dead," Ana insisted, smiling at his instant psychoanalysis. Although, she did, like several other models she knew, feel guilty about propagating an image of perfection that was, frankly, a lie. She had been honest in several interviews about the hours spent being made-up and then, if the subsequent photographs weren't up to par, being airbrushed to make them perfect.

"You're a man of substance, a man whose life means much more than the pursuit of self-gratification. To me, what you do is inspiring, saving peoples' jobs, keeping families together. Being a model doesn't compare to that."

"You have helped raise millions of dollars for New York City's homeless," Erik reminded her.

"Yes, as a result of modeling I've been able to help others. That's a plus. In my opinion, the only true benefit. It's not enough, though. You need a woman who is equal to you in every way."

Erik laughed softly. "You're already my equal in every way."

Ana took a sip of her wine and swallowed. "There's always room for improvement."

Erik raised her hand to his lips and kissed her fingers. "You do realize that this is your personal little quirk, and I wholeheartedly disagree with your assessment?"

"If that's business talk for you think I'm a little nuts to think this way, then, yeah, I do," Ana said, smiling.

Their waiter approached at that instance, and they ordered dinner. After the waiter left them alone, Ana changed the subject with, "So, are we going running in the park tomorrow morning?" They had a standing date on Saturday mornings to run in Central Park if both of them were in the city.

"No, I'm sorry, but tomorrow I'll be driving to Bridgeport for the weekend." Erik sighed. Some of the people he'd had to negotiate with over the years had made some strange stipulations before signing on the dotted line. However Leo Barone's invitation to spend the weekend with his family took the prize. Barone owned a shoe factory that Whitaker Enterprises was in the process of purchasing. Barone stated that he wanted to meet the head of Whitaker Enterprises in a social setting before signing over his company, and the people who worked for him, to him. The biggest hitch in the negotiations had been Barone's concern for his employees once he was no longer their boss.

According to Barone, lawyers were fine for ironing out the legalities. However nothing compared to spending time with a person to get a real feel for what kind of man he was. Erik relayed all of this to Ana after which she responded with a smile, "Do you think he'd mind another guest for the weekend?"

"Of course not," said Erik, smiling as if that was his plan all along. "I told him I would try to convince my lady friend to accompany me."

"Is that what I am—your lady friend?" Ana asked, her eyes sparkling with mischief.

"You're a lady and you're my friend," Erik replied, playing along.

"Could you drop the 'friend' part and refer to me as your lady from now on?" she asked, eyes sparkling with humor.

"As far as I'm concerned you've been my lady for quite some time now," Erik told her, looking into her eyes with sensual intensity. "I was just waiting for you to come to that conclusion."

"Then remember this date," Ana told him, "because the wait is over."

With that, she leaned in and kissed him. Because of where they were Ana held back, even though it took some strength to do so. Erik's mouth was one of the things she liked best about him. His lips were beautifully formed, and when he smiled, showing those even white teeth, she got all jittery inside. Each time she gave him a peck on the cheek she always entertained the notion of kissing him full on the lips. It had never happened before. Erik respected her wishes to keep things platonic. He'd not even "accidentally" missed her cheek, grazing her mouth—not once.

She glanced at his mouth now and made a vow: *this night will not end until I get my fill of those lips!*

Chapter 2

"Let me drive!" Ana exclaimed, running her hand along the driver's side of Erik's sleek, black Corvette the next morning. Erik couldn't hold back a laugh her face was so animated with pure delight.

She looked fresh and stylish in jeans, a cotton shirt open at the neck, a thick brown jacket to guard against the cold and brown suede boots. Her thick hair was pulled back in a ponytail. Erik also wore jeans, but had paired them with athletic shoes, an MIT T-shirt, and his favorite black leather jacket.

"I've barely had her out on the road myself since I bought her," he said, chuckling and holding the car keys high above his head out of her reach. Ana pressed her chest to his as she stretched on tiptoe, trying her best to snatch the keys from his grasp.

"Come on, I'll be good, I promise. No more than, five, ten miles over the speed limit."

"This is not Europe, and we don't have an autobahn," Erik reminded her as he handed over the keys. She had him at a disadvantage. Her close proximity—her breasts against his chest, the subtle erotic, utterly feminine scent she exuded—were causing an all too familiar physical reaction in him. Better to relent and let her drive.

Ana clutched the keys in her hand and let out a whoop. "You choose the music, and let's roll!"

Erik got in and buckled up. He watched as Ana slid into the driver's side, automatically adjusted the seat to her proportions, then fastened her seat belt.

She turned and smiled at him as she turned the key in the ignition. He could have sworn she got pleasure from the purring of the engine. He'd never known a woman who loved to drive as much as she did. He had to admit, she was a good driver. Yes, there was that one time when they got pulled over for speeding, but even the officer stated that she hadn't been driving recklessly, just over the speed limit. He had let her off with a warning.

Ana consulted the GPS and pulled into the early-morning Manhattan traffic. "Tell me more about the Barones."

Erik was riffling through the CDs. He selected a Howlin' Wolf album and put it in the CD player. "Well, the business was started by Leo's grandfather, Alphonse, in the early 1900s. He and his wife, Lucia, were from Salerno, Italy. Leo's father, Leo, Senior, took over in the sixties and left the business to Leo when he died in the eighties."

"Doesn't Leo have any children to leave the business to?" asked Ana. It made no sense to her that Leo would sell the family business, even if he were having financial troubles, when the tradition in the Barone family was for the children to inherit the business. The Corellis' clothing-manufacturing business was also an inherited family business.

"They had a son, but the boy was killed in a diving accident when he was nineteen."

"That's terrible," said Ana sympathetically.

"They still have a daughter. She's sixteen now."

"What a blessing. She doesn't show any interest in the business?"

"From what I'm told, she's more into soccer. Her team was the state champs last year."

"You seem to know a lot about them."

"I make it my business to know whom I'm dealing with," Erik said matter-of-factly. "Besides, Leo likes to talk about his family."

"What about his wife?"

"He met her in Rome when he visited the old country for the first time, is how he put it. It was love at first sight. He learned Italian in order to communicate with her."

"You mean he's Italian and didn't speak Italian?"

"Italian was the language his grandfather spoke, and

he never quite mastered. But when he met Teresa she refused to speak English so he had to learn it."

"Smart woman," said Ana laughing softly.

"Yes, he later found out she could speak English all along."

"Very smart woman," she added as she nodded her head to the beat of the music. "Who *is* that?"

"Howlin' Wolf," Erik told her. "He was known for classic Chicago blues. Like Muddy Waters."

He knew Ana was slowly working her way through American blues singers. She loved the gutbucket blues the best, the rough-and-ready singers who got under your skin with the emotion in their voices.

"He's got a gritty, sexy tone to his voice," she said. "I could listen to him all night."

Erik grinned, "Are you blushing?"

"No," she denied, eyes on the road. "Tell me more about him."

"He was a big guy," Erik said, "six-six and almost three hundred pounds."

"He *sounds* big," Ana said.

"He and Muddy Waters were rivals. I don't know why, exactly, but they reportedly didn't like each other much."

"Probably a professional rivalry," Ana suggested. "They competed for jobs, maybe record deals, maybe even women."

"They probably didn't have to compete for women. Women love musicians. There were undoubtedly enough to go around."

"Who knows, maybe they were in love with the same woman," Ana countered. "Men have feuded over women since the beginning of time. Remember Helen of Troy?"

Erik laughed. "The blues *is* usually about a broken romance," he said. "You could be right."

They talked about the blues and listened to it the entire trip. It was nearly noon when Ana turned onto the long driveway that led to the Barone house, a three-story Tudor-style mansion on the outskirts of Bridgeport. There were three other late-model cars parked on the circular drive.

Ana parked the Corvette and turned off the engine. Shy by nature, she was always a little apprehensive about meeting new people. "Here we are," she said to Erik hesitantly.

Before they could get out of the car, the Barones, looking relaxed in their casual weekend clothes and warm jackets, came out of the house, welcoming smiles on their faces.

"Oh my God, it *is* Ana Corelli!" Julianna Barone cried, sprinting to the driver's side and pulling open the door. "When Daddy said Mr. Whitaker was bringing his lady friend, Ana Corelli, I thought to myself, 'Not *the* Ana Corelli!' But it *is* you!"

Ana got out and was immediately enveloped in Julianna's arms. Ana hugged her back. Then they peered into each other's faces. "It's good to meet you…" Ana began.

"Julianna. I'm sorry. Where're my manners?" Julianna said.

"I was wondering that myself," said Teresa Barone. She was in her early fifties, five-six and curvy with tanned skin. Her dark brown hair was cut short and framed her lovely face nicely.

"This is my mom, Teresa," said Julianna.

"Welcome to our home," said Teresa in Italian, having noticed Ana's accent. "It's a pleasure to meet you, Ana."

Ana smiled, loving the way the language tripped off the other woman's tongue. It had been a while since anyone other than her family had spoken in Italian to her. She answered in Italian and soon the two of them were speaking rapidly in the language. Teresa took her by the arm and led her inside with Leo, Erik and Julianna following.

"Forgive her," said Leo to Erik, commenting on the fact that his wife had totally ignored him in favor of Ana. "It isn't often she meets someone who speaks her native tongue as fluently as she does. It goes to her head. How was your trip?"

Erik told him they'd had a pleasant drive. He looked around him, at the beautiful house and acres of greenery. "Is that a stable?" he asked about the outlying building east of the house.

"It is," Leo told him. He shaded his eyes with a hand as he looked across the field at the well-kept stables. "In good weather, Teresa and I ride every day. We're trying to interest Julianna."

"But I'm scared of horses," Julianna finished for her father. She smiled up at Erik. She was taller than her mother, but had the same chestnut hair. However hers was long and fell nearly to her waist in waves. Her complexion was also somewhere between her mother's dark skin and her father's fairer skin. She and her father were nearly the same height at around five-nine.

She and Leo stood aside as Erik retrieved his and Ana's luggage from the car's trunk.

"Yes, well, I've never gotten used to them myself," Erik told her. "My father raises horses. These days he calls himself a gentleman farmer, and horses are one of his obsessions."

"Finally," Julianna said, "someone else who doesn't think horses are the noble beasts my parents think they are. Those things are big! They've got hard hooves and they bite!"

"They don't bite," Leo said, chuckling. "Well, I've never been bitten by one, anyway."

"You've been lucky," his daughter said.

Leo suggested they put the luggage in the foyer closet until after lunch.

By the time they got into the kitchen where Teresa had led Ana, the two women were already putting lunch on the table while chattering away.

Teresa looked up at her husband when they came into the room. "Ana tells me that her mother is Natalie Davis-Corelli. Do you remember we saw her onstage in Rome over twenty-five years ago?"

"I do," said Leo. He regarded Ana with an amazed

look on his face. "I didn't care much for opera at that time. It was your mother who changed that for me. I'd never heard a voice so pure, so clear, or so emotional. Is she still singing?"

"She performs on special occasions," Ana told him, "but mostly she teaches voice lessons."

After years of singing, she gets a lot of joy out of helping other singers reach their full potential.

Leo, Erik and Julianna sat on stools around the granite-topped island in the middle of the large stylish kitchen while Teresa and Ana put the dishes Teresa had prepared earlier in the center of the island. The smells to Ana were reminiscent of home.

"You come from a family of musicians," Leo said to Ana. He smiled at his wife. "Being married to an opera expert, I've picked up a little knowledge over the years." He returned his attention to Ana. "If your mother is Natalie Davis-Corelli that means your grandmother was Renata Corelli."

"Yes," Ana said, pleased to know he knew of her grandmother who had died several years ago and was still sorely missed.

"I never saw her perform live," Leo said regrettably. "But I've seen her in films. She was amazing."

Ana couldn't think of her grandmother without getting a little choked up. She swallowed a lump in her throat, and softly said, "She was happiest when she was performing."

Leo continued, excitedly. "No wonder your brother is a composer, his mother and his grandmother—two world-renowned singers. It was in his blood. What about you, do you have musical talent?"

Ana laughed shortly. "Not a bit. Musical talent skipped me and my sister, Sophia. Neither of us can carry a tune. Or play an instrument with any proficiency. We went into fashion, like our father. Sophia works with him in his clothing business and I became a model."

"You sound so modest," Teresa said, smiling warmly. "You did more than just became a model. You're very successful at it."

"I've been lucky," Ana admitted.

"And very hard-working," Erik put in fondly.

"There's no substitution for hard work," Leo said. He gave his daughter a meaningful look. "That's what I've been trying to drive home with our soccer fanatic here. You have to burn the midnight oil to get anywhere."

"We were state champs this year," Julianna said a bit defensively.

"Yes, but a girl can't live by soccer alone," her father countered. "In order to get into a good college, you'll need more than just a good athletic record. You're too single minded. What about academics and other extracurricular activities? You have to be well-rounded."

"Ana was single-minded in her career," Julianna pointed out. "If she hadn't been focused on becoming the best model she could be, she wouldn't be where she is today."

"Ana?" Leo said, obviously looking for an ally in this argument. "Tell us, please, is that true?"

"My parents insisted I get a college degree," Ana told Julianna. "I have a bachelor's degree in business. And I've been taking art classes for years."

"See?" cried Teresa. "Beauty and brains!"

"That is so cool," said Julianna. "Don't take this the wrong way but I always thought of models as self-absorbed airheads."

"You can find self-absorbed airheads in any career," Ana said, to which everyone laughed.

They all sat down and soon were enjoying a lunch of Teresa's native southern Italian cuisine—a seafood soup with fresh tomatoes and savory herbs, hot crusty bread and peach gelato for dessert.

"You're a great cook," Ana said to Teresa. "This soup reminds me of my father's seafood soup."

"That's why I married her," Leo said cheerfully.

Teresa, who was sitting beside her husband, reached over and tousled his too-long dark hair. He was graying at the temples, which gave him a sexy, rugged appearance as far as she was concerned. She adored him and it was reflected in the way her eyes caressed his face. "One of the reasons, anyway," she said, then winked at him.

"Behave," their daughter said with a laugh. "We've got company." Then she turned to Erik and said, "Mr. Whitaker, Dad says you want to buy the family business. I searched your company on Google and found out you've bought several companies that were having problems."

"I don't think this is the time to discuss business,"

Leo said abruptly, obviously surprised by his daughter's comment.

"Dad, isn't that why you invited Mr. Whitaker and Ana here this weekend?"

"Please, call me Erik," said Erik with a smile.

"What I wanted to say," Julianna continued calmly, "is that if Dad is going to sell the family business, I hope it's to a company like yours. You're environmentally responsible. You have a good record when it comes to keeping the employees who're dependent on the companies you acquire to make a living." She regarded her father. "I know you're worried about that, Dad. That's why I decided to do a little research. Not that you haven't already done that, but I wanted to reassure myself. I know you think I don't have any interest in the business, but I do. I keep my ears and eyes open."

Leo looked at her with such pride that, seeing his expression, Teresa got emotional and had to wipe a tear away. "My baby," she said in a whisper.

"Dad, I'm sorry if it seems I'm being disrespectful, I don't mean to. But if you remember, I've tried to talk to you about the business for weeks now and you always tell me not to worry about it."

Leo didn't know what to say. He thought Julianna lived in her own world of soccer, her friends and the internet, in that order. That she had made an effort to find out what sort of company Whitaker Enterprises was made him wonder if perhaps he'd been too quick to call it a day where the company was concerned. Maybe there was a Barone who looked forward to running it one day. If he redoubled his efforts there was a possibility that with an infusion of new ideas, and investors, the Barone Shoe Company, whose slogan had always been Quality Italian Shoes Made in America, could remain in the family.

"I'm listening," he said to his daughter.

"Before you sell the family business," Julianna said, "I just want to make sure that's what you really want to do, or is it because Leo, Jr.'s in heaven and you don't think a woman could run the company after you retire?" She was all seriousness, her gaze unwavering. "Or maybe there's something you're not telling me— like you're sick and that's why you're selling the company and retiring at sixty."

Leo got up and pulled his daughter into his arms. "No, sweetheart, no to both of your questions," he said. "I know that if you put your mind to it, you're capable of anything. I just didn't know you were interested in working with me. And I'm as healthy as a horse!"

Julianna laughed. "You know I don't like horses."

"Okay, I'm as healthy as David Beckham," said Leo.

"That's better," said Julianna.

"Let's sit," said Leo. Once they were both seated, Leo turned to Erik. "It looks like we have a lot to talk about this weekend, after all. I was ready to sign, but now I'm having sudden misgivings."

Erik had been listening with interest. This wasn't the first time a deal had come this close to being finalized and had fallen through...if that's where this was going. He had learned to roll with the punches. "I'm sure we can work something out that will be agreeable to both of us. We're not in the business of trying to force anyone to sell. We only approached you because you had decided that selling might be an option out of your financial crunch. However we're willing to work with you. If you want to remain the company's CEO and train Julianna to eventually replace you with us as an investor, you can go that way. It's your decision. We like Barone Shoes and we think you can once again be a major competitor in the shoe market."

Leo regarded his wife. "Do you think we can postpone our months-long tour of Italy a few more years until Julianna's ready to assume control of the business?"

Teresa in turn regarded Julianna. "Baby, you're only sixteen. How can you be so sure you want to run the business one day?"

"Because it's my family," Julianna said firmly. "I'm a Barone. Like Grandpa and Dad before me. Plus, I feel a connection with Leo, Jr.—as if we'd be doing it together. I know I never knew him, but I love him anyway."

Teresa had tears in her eyes when she told her husband, "Okay, I can wait a few years. Give her a chance."

"Let's talk about taking you all on as investors," Leo said to Erik and offered him his hand across the table. Erik took it and firmly shook it.

"I'm sure we can work something out," Erik agreed.

After lunch, Erik and Leo, went into the family library and hammered out a deal that would give Whitaker Enterprises a quarter interest in Barone Shoes in exchange for a healthy loan. Erik felt confident that Whitaker Enterprises had made a good investment. And Leo felt he could trust Whitaker Enterprises to support them, but not interfere in the day-to-day running of Barone Shoes. However, Erik made one stipulation: Barone Shoes had to submit to Whitaker Enterprises' efficiency experts and accountants in order to insure that the company was being run in the black from now on. Whitaker Enterprises didn't invest in a losing proposition. They wouldn't be the powerhouse they were today if they did. Leo wholeheartedly agreed.

The two men stood and shook on it. "Since that's settled, Ana and I should be getting back on the road," Erik said.

"No, please stay the night," Leo said. He grinned. "We had planned a party for you tonight and invited some of the employees so they could meet you, the new owner. Now they can meet the new investor. Stay, won't you?"

Erik would like nothing better than to spend the rest of the day and the weekend with Ana. After last night, he was looking forward to some alone time with her. However, Ana had been promised a weekend in Connecticut and he hated disappointing her. Plus, it might be a good idea to meet some of Leo's employees. "All right," he said. "I'd like that."

Chapter 3

"Are you disappointed things didn't turn out as you thought they would?" Ana asked Erik when they were alone on the common balcony of the guestrooms Teresa had shown them to after Erik's talk with Leo. Earlier Teresa had discreetly asked Ana if she and Erik wanted to share a room and Ana had told her their relationship hadn't advanced that far yet, to which Teresa had smiled and said, "How refreshing."

"It's never wise to anticipate the outcome of a deal," Erik said, his smile denoting he wasn't that broken up about it. He closed the space between them and pulled her into his arms. Ana smiled up at him and said, "It's cold out here." She snuggled closer and breathed in the enticing male scent of him, which was like an aphrodisiac to her senses. Looking into his eyes, she said, "If

I've appeared a bit distant all day, it's because I can't forget that kiss last night."

He'd taken her home after dinner and had come in for coffee. Among the things they had in common was an addiction to caffeine. Neither was bothered by sleeplessness if they indulged before bed. Ana had gone into the kitchen of her loft to make the coffee and Erik, as he often did, followed her. While she was tiptoeing to reach the container of beans on the top shelf of the cabinet, he was admiring her backside. Ana turned around and caught him looking. "Is that something you do often or is it a new development?" she asked playfully.

"It's pretty much a habit," Erik confessed.

Ana set the container on the counter and faced him, her expression aghast. "You mean to tell me that for the last three years you've been looking at my bottom without my knowledge?"

"Oh, I think you knew," Erik said as he slipped his arm about her waist and pressed her to his muscular chest, smiling all the while. He lowered his head and inhaled her unique fragrance. She'd noticed that he liked doing that, as though the smell of her skin gave him sensual pleasure. It turned her on, too.

Her body immediately reacted to his. Her nipples grew hard, and she became moist between her legs. It was a heady, all-too-erotic sensation that was so delicious she let out a soft sigh. She looked at his lips. He was smiling and his white teeth, coupled with those juicy lips, looked so inviting that she threw her arms around his neck and kissed him. Erik didn't need any further provocation. Her lips were soft and her mouth so sweet that before he knew it he had lifted her body and her legs wrapped around him in a bid to get even closer. Their tongues danced gently at first and found the encounter so pleasing that the kiss deepened and soon they were both sounding as though they were consuming something extremely tasty as, no doubt, they were. Erik, as the one who had most of the physical strength between them, knew that he had to back off before things got out of hand. Ana wasn't ready for things to go any further than a kiss but it was their first real kiss and, heaven help him, if her kisses were this good, what would sex be like with her?

It was Ana who came up for air first and looked him in the eyes. She pressed her cheek to his. "Why haven't you kissed me before now?"

"I've been a fool," Erik said, and kissed her again.

Ana pulled his shirt out of his waistband so that she could run her hands over his hot skin. Another new experience since friends didn't routinely touch one another's naked bodies. Her feverish mind thought back. Yes, she'd seen Erik in a swimsuit on a couple occasions. Once when they had flown to Barbados for the weekend with his sister, Belana, and her husband, Nick, and another time when they'd taken a dip in the pool at his parents' house in Connecticut. He was in great shape. Cut from all the running and weightlifting he did on a daily basis. Ana was not nearly as disciplined. She liked running with Erik on Saturday mornings, but walking was more her taste. All this was going through her mind while the man of her dreams was kissing her, and she thought she must be neurotic to be thinking of anything other than the taste of his mouth and the warm, solid feel of his body touching hers. It was fear of change that stood in the way of her truly enjoying Erik.

What would she do if he made love to her and lost interest, just as that actor who would remain nameless had done? It would kill her—she realized at that instant in her kitchen, she adored this man. She loved him in a way she had never thought to love a man, completely. Until Erik she thought of men as enigmas whom women were doomed to never fully understand. However Erik had proved that theory a lie. She understood him. She knew, for example, that even though he denied it he had an abandonment issue with his mother. It's true that his mother had come back into his life briefly last year, but by that time the damage had been done. And she wasn't in his life long before she revealed she had a terminal illness. Only weeks later she had died with all her children holding her hands, the very children she had walked away from. No one came away from that without emotional scarring.

Erik had never let himself get close to anyone before Ana. He jokingly said it was because he'd just never found the right woman. Ana believed it was because he was afraid of being abandoned yet again by a woman he loved. This, Ana, thought last night in her kitchen, put a great deal of pressure on her. She would never dream of hurting him, but what if she did hurt him in spite of every effort not to? She was only human.

It was soon after this thought ran through her mind that Erik had tipped her chin toward him and said, "Let's not waste any more time than we already have. I love you, Ana. I believe I've loved you since the first time we met."

Tears instantly sprang to Ana's eyes. "I love you, too!" She hugged him tightly. "I love you so much that I'm afraid of my feelings for you."

He kissed her forehead. "Afraid? What do you mean?"

"What we have is perfect in a sense. You're my best friend, the person I confide in, aside from my own family. What if that changes? What if becoming lovers changes us?"

Erik laughed. "If anything it'll enhance how we already feel about each other." He became somber. "It's that actor, isn't it? The one who broke your heart after you'd slept with him? Ana, you're not guilty of doing anything to warrant his behavior. Some men are bastards and will always be bastards. He's one of them. I'm sure you're not the only woman he's treated that way."

"Maybe I'm not good in bed," Ana said miserably.

Erik held her by the shoulders and looked deeply in her eyes. "That's the most ludicrous statement I've ever heard." He smiled as he pulled her into his arms. "One day, my sweet Ana, you and I are going to make love, and you're going to know without a doubt that you are very, very good in bed and maybe the couch, the kitchen table and the shower, too."

Ana laughed and cried. "Someday? Why not this day, this night?"

"Because sex for the first time is an event," Erik said. "It'll be remembered forever and you don't want to mess with forever. We've waited this long, we can wait awhile longer."

Now, as they stood in each other's arms on the Barone's balcony, Ana gazed up at him and said, "It's just as well we didn't make love last night because I would want you again tonight and it would be awkward making love under the Barones' roof."

"We'd be very quiet," Erik joked.

"I doubt it," Ana countered.

Later, at the party, Erik spent most of the time fielding questions from Leo Barone's employees who wanted to know more about Whitaker Enterprises. It was apparent to him that they were grateful to be retaining their jobs in these hard economic times. So many people were out of jobs and finding it difficult to find another. They almost made him feel like some kind of hero for offering assistance to Barone Shoes, a feeling he fervently declined.

"I should be thanking you," he told them. "Leo has built a wonderful business and you've contributed to the quality of the product he produces. Without loyal, hardworking employees, no business would survive. Or be able to build a reputation investors like myself notice when we're looking to invest in someone."

Leo had stepped up and said, "That's a long way of

saying he wouldn't have been interested if we didn't make a quality product."

Everyone laughed, but Erik was happy he'd gotten his point across and from that moment on during the evening, business was not discussed. The topics stayed on golf and sports teams.

Meanwhile in another section of the great room, the women and children were gathered around Ana who was quickly making sketches of the children in charcoal. She didn't go anywhere without her sketch pad and the children were taking great delight in her swift manner of drawing their likenesses. Since it was only a few days from Halloween, Teresa had suggested that the children come in costumes and, now, Ana was drawing the image of a six-year-old African-American girl dressed as a fairy princess. The mother of the little girl stood behind Ana on one side, and Julianna stood on the other.

"You're very good," the mother said, smiling broadly. "You even captured the mischievous expression in Nikki's eyes."

Julianna laughed. "That's our Nikki to a T." She had babysat Nikki on occasion and knew the little girl was a handful.

Ana, sitting on a straight-backed chair directly in front of Nikki, smiled warmly. "She's adorable."

Finished with Nikki's portrait, she handed the finished product to Nikki's mother. Nikki climbed off her chair and spontaneously kissed Ana on the cheek. "Thank you," she said.

"Well," Ana said, laughing softly. "That's the first time I've ever been paid in kisses for my work. Thank you, Nikki."

With Nikki's portrait, Ana had drawn all four children who had attended the party with their parents. Not to be outdone, Teresa asked sweetly, "Would you draw my baby now?"

Julianna immediately took umbrage with being called a baby. "Mother, I'm not a baby!"

"You're my baby, and always will be. Get used to it," Teresa returned. "Now sit down and let Ana draw you. It's not every day that you get to have your picture drawn by an artist of her caliber." She smiled at Ana. "Don't you dare forget to phone and tell me when and where your show is going to take place."

"I won't," Ana promised. She met Julianna's gaze.

Julianna grinned and sat down. Then she crossed her eyes. "Will this do?"

Ana laughed. "Sure if that's how you want to be remembered."

Julianna uncrossed her eyes and gave Ana a genuine smile. "You're sneaky. I like that."

The men wandered over and stood admiring the sketch as it formed on Ana's pad. Leo joked, "Give her horns. I swear she's a little devil sometimes."

Teresa playfully hit Leo on the backside. "If anyone's a little devil in this family, it's you."

Erik stood back and watched Ana, how easily she was handling being the center of attention even though she insisted she was shy. Whether it was on the runway or in a room full of children, she always seemed comfortable in her own skin to him.

When Ana finished the portrait Julianna held it in her hands, admiring it. "You even managed to make me pretty," she said in awe.

"I just drew what I saw," Ana said truthfully.

Teresa took the drawing from Julianna. "This is going in a place of honor." She bent and kissed Ana on the cheek. "Thank you, Ana." She had to wipe away a tear.

Leo, feeling things were getting maudlin, bellowed, "The night's still young. Who's up for some virtual golf?"

The men were all for that, and once again the guests were divided by sex with the men heading downstairs to the finished basement where Leo's entertainment center was set up.

Teresa led the women to the kitchen where they indulged in coffee and delicious desserts the caterer had provided for the party. The children were in their own special heaven in the den playing video games.

Ana sat between two women in their thirties, one African-American, the other a blonde with dark roots who kept gazing at Ana as if she wanted to ask her something but couldn't muster up the nerve to do so. Ana smiled at her and said, "Your husband is the plant's manager, right?"

They'd all introduced themselves earlier. Ana recalled her husband—a tall, heavyset fellow with a ruddy complexion—was very tender with their son who looked about three.

"Yeah, Ben," said the woman. "And I'm Sasha."

"Your son's so sweet. I have a niece his age. She lives in Italy. I miss her so much."

"What's her name?"

"Ari…Ariana," said Ana. "Now she has a baby brother and she's having a hard time getting used to him. She told her mom to take him back to the hospital and trade him in for a puppy."

The other women who had been listening to their conversation laughed.

"Yes, older kids do sometimes take a while to get used to a new addition," Teresa said after swallowing a mouthful of pecan pie. "When Julianna was three months old Leo, Jr. once wrapped her in a blanket and left her on a neighbor's doorstep. Luckily we were living in a close-knit neighborhood at that time, and the neighbors saw him do it and immediately phoned me. He only got away with it because Leo was at work and I was in the shower. Of course when Leo, Jr. got older he absolutely loved his sister and doted on her. Or maybe it was guilt that made him so protective of her later on." She laughed, remembering her son fondly. "Julianna adored him from birth. She would follow him around like a lost puppy looking for a scrap of food."

Ana supposed the woman who went and pulled Teresa into her arms for a firm hug was an old friend. A sympathetic and knowing look passed between them and the woman said, "He adored her. You could see it every time you saw them together."

"Yes," another woman agreed.

Soon others were relating Leo, Jr. stories. It was obvious to Ana that the employees of Barone Shoes were more than employees to the Barones, they were old friends. It made her feel happy that Leo had decided not to sell the company after all.

On Sunday Ana and Erik got back to the city in the early afternoon. After dropping Ana off at her loft and making plans to meet for dinner later, Erik continued on to his apartment.

When Erik walked into this apartment, bags in hand, he dropped them in the foyer and walked back to the kitchen to get a bottle of water from the fridge. After drinking quickly he turned and went into the home office. The blinking light of the answering machine on the desk was like a beacon to him. Only his friends and family used his home phone number. Business calls went straight to his cell phone. He liked keeping them separate because on weekends, he ignored the office. He would never, however, ignore his friends and family.

He listened to the first message. It was his father, John. He began with a tired sigh, so Erik instinctively knew the message would be about his grandmother, Drusilla. No one could get under his father's skin quite like his grandmother. "Hey, son, your grandmother took another tumble today. She's so hardheaded. We keep telling her to use her cane but she insists she doesn't need it every day, just when, and these are her words, 'I'm feeling wobbly.'" John sighed heavily again. "It's Friday night and they're keeping her in the hospital overnight for observation. A fall can be dangerous for an eighty-two-year-old."

Let her be all right, Erik prayed as he continued listening.

"No need to come home, though," his father said. "She's fine. It's my nerves that are frayed." He laughed. "Thank God for Izzie. She remained calm and handled everything with her usual quiet efficiency." Izzie was Isobel, Erik's stepmother. She and his father had been married for three years and still behaved like newlyweds. Erik loved and admired her for how happy she'd made his father, who deserved a little happiness after all the heartache he'd experienced when Mari had left him for a French choreographer.

He dialed the house in New Haven, Connecticut and waited. Isobel answered with, "Hi, sweetie. I hope John's message didn't upset you. Dru's back home and is doing well. How're you?"

Erik smiled. Isobel rarely answered with hello. She anticipated your needs and got right into the conversation. "I'm fine, Mom, and how are you?" Both he and Belana referred to Isobel as "Mom." They'd known her for years before she and their father had fallen in love and gotten married. She was the mother of one of Belana's best friends, Elle, and consequently they were part of the same social circle. What's more, Isobel, as far as Belana and Erik were concerned, had earned the title of "Mom" since she loved them like her own even though they were not related by blood.

He could hear the smile in her voice when she said, "Just great. We're all sitting around the kitchen table having lunch. Would you like to speak with your father or Drusilla?"

"Put Her Majesty on, please."

When Drusilla got on the phone he could hear her clearing her throat. "Where are you that you can't come see about your poor old grandmother?"

"Who would that be?" Erik asked, "Because you are apparently as young and spry as ever! I'm told you don't think you need to use your cane anymore. Is that right?"

"It makes me look old and decrepit."

"You're too vain. What would you prefer? To look your age, or break a hip, or worse?" he asked, being careful not to raise his voice.

"I'd rather look good," was Drusilla's petulant reply. "What does it matter if I go out with a broken hip or not? The Grim Reaper has my number. I should have the right to choose how I live the rest of my life. After more than eighty years, I've earned it!"

Erik sighed. She had a point. Eighty-two years on earth should allow her certain privileges. He'd have to guilt her into behaving herself.

"Yes, you've earned the right to flip off the Grim Reaper if you want to. But, while you're tempting fate, what about the rest of us who would like to have you around a bit longer? What about Dad and Belana? What about those great-grandchildren you're always urging

Belana and me to have? And hurry up about it, too? Shouldn't they get the honor of having you as a cantankerous great-grandma? What do you say to that?"

"You should've been a lawyer," Drusilla groused. She laughed. "Okay, I'll use the damn cane from now on."

"Language!" Erik heard his dad admonish his grandmother before bursting into laughter himself. His dad must have taken the phone from his grandmother. "Okay, son, whatever you said seems to have worked. She looks dutifully repentant, *for now.*"

Erik couldn't help laughing. Both he and his father knew it was only a matter of time before Drusilla found another outlet for her indefatigable spirit to get her into trouble.

"By the way, Dad, Ana and I are dating," Eric said after he'd gotten his laughter under control.

With his usual aplomb, John said without missing a beat, "Haven't you always been dating?"

"Technically, we were just friends."

"Seriously?" said John. "For two years you and Ana have been platonic friends?" He sounded so disbelieving that Erik started laughing again.

"Yes, seriously," he assured his father.

"I know you said you were just friends, but I never imagined that two young, healthy people like you and Ana were actually keeping your hands to yourselves. Son, I was just happy you had someone like Ana in your life. Mother, will you stop that!"

Drusilla said hastily, "It's about damn time!" Then she was gone.

John, sounding exasperated, said, "That's wonderful news. Now I've got to go, your grandmother's has had too much excitement for one day."

Erik hung up the phone and listened to the remaining messages on the machine. None were pressing, so he wandered into this bedroom and began changing his clothes. He felt restless and a long jog would go a long way in relaxing him and focusing his mind. His father's reaction to the news of him and Ana dating made him wonder if the rest of his family believed the two of them had been more than friends all the time.

Wasn't it possible for a man and a woman to be just friends? Surely he'd proven they could. Then again, even if his behavior had been above reproach, his thoughts definitely hadn't been. Not being able to express his feelings for Ana in a sexual way had made him very resourceful. Running helped, as did staying extremely busy. Now that they'd admitted their feelings for each other, and sex was sure to follow, he hoped he'd be able to make love to Ana without scaring the poor girl by howling like a beast or something else equally embarrassing. He was only a man.

Running clothes and shoes on, he grabbed the apartment key he kept in the foyer table on the way out the door. I hope Ana isn't overanalyzing everything like I am, he thought as he closed the door behind him.

Chapter 4

"**I**'m freaking out!" Ana cried, trying to control the panic in her voice. Her sister, Sophia, in Milan was half asleep. She usually slept in on Sunday and it was still quite early in her part of the world.

Ana was lying in bed with her back against the headboard and her long legs stretched out. Sophia was under the covers with her husband, Matteo, who was snugly pressed against her backside, gently snoring. It would take more than the shrill ringing of a phone to wake him.

Sophia yawned before replying, "Yes, I do detect a little freaking out on your part," she said. "But that's to be expected since you've let a guy as hot as Erik slip through your fingers for as long as you have. I was beginning to doubt your sanity."

That comment made Ana smile. Leave it to her practical sister to point out the obvious. "It's not like I'm jumping into bed with every man who shows interest," she said in her defense. "You know how inexperienced I am."

"I know your only experience was a negative one and you're not going to fully appreciate how truly bad it was until you have a good encounter with a man who knows what he's doing in bed. Then, what Jack Russo did to you will feel like a slight glitch in your very satisfying love life. Oh, sorry, we aren't supposed to be saying his name. Jack Russo, Jack Russo, Jack Russo. By saying his name you take some of the power out of it. You know the only reason he dropped you was because he had that actress waiting in the wings and she had more money and clout than you. I hate it when bastards like that just run over a woman's feelings. You know, if I had been anywhere in the vicinity he would be missing his most vital organ right now."

Ana giggled. "Matteo must be sleeping very hard not to react to that comment."

Sophia giggled, too. "Yeah, he's out. Your nephew had both of us up late last night."

"Oh, I'm sorry for interrupting your much needed rest. What was wrong with my nephew?"

"Teething," said Sophia. "Breast-feeding is becoming dangerous."

Ana sighed sympathetically. "Thinking of switching him to a bottle?"

"I'm going to have to," said Sophia. "Besides, according to his doctor he's gotten all the good nutrients from breast milk that he needs at six months."

Remembering the conversation about firstborns not accepting new sisters and brothers, Ana said, "How is Renata handling being a big sister?"

"She loves him, calls him her baby," said Sophia. She yawned again.

"Look, I'd better let you go," said Ana. "I just wanted to hear a calm voice."

"And you called *me?*" joked Sophia. "Mom is the only one with a calm voice in this family."

"Don't mention our conversation to them, okay? I'll tell them when the time's right."

"You *are* coming home for Christmas?" asked Sophia.

Ana always went home for Christmas, which was celebrated with all the trimmings by the Corellis.

"I don't know yet," Ana said truthfully. "With these new developments in my life I might want to go somewhere romantic with my man." The thought excited her. "I'll have to let you know."

"Now you sound like the idea of you and Erik as a couple is taking root," Sophia told her, pleased with the confidence in her sister's voice. "Okay, sis, talk to you later."

"Love you," said Ana.

"Love you!" Sophia replied.

Ana hung up the phone and got up. She glanced at the clock on the nightstand. It was nearly three. She and Erik were going to dinner at eight. She had plenty of time to work on a painting before getting dressed for their date.

She'd changed her clothes upon entering the loft and now she was in comfortable sweats and an oversize T-shirt. In thick white socks she padded over to her "studio"—a section of the loft next to two floor-to-ceiling windows, which let in a lot of natural light.

Although she had finished all of the paintings that were to be included in the upcoming show, she invariably had a work in progress on the easel. She removed the cloth and peered down at the half-finished portrait of Drusilla. She had sketched Drusilla so many times she knew every line and plane of her beloved face. Drusilla had never been a large woman. Not even five feet tall, she was also small boned. Because of her age, the skin on her face was thin and the bones were sharply delineated. Ana noticed things like that. Her artist's eye adored the bone structure of human beings. That's why she felt most comfortable painting portraits. She did some landscapes, too, but not many. Nothing was more beautiful to her than the human form. In Italy, when she first started taking lessons, her instructor had encouraged her to study anatomy. He gave her a battered copy of *Grey's Anatomy* and she had studied it from cover to cover, her teenaged mind becoming obsessed with the human body. Now when she looked at people she didn't just see their outward appearance, but their bone structure and consequently she saw beauty in every face she observed.

Two hours later, she was still constructing Drusilla's face on the canvas. Even though she'd been doing this for years it still amazed her, and felt somewhat miraculous, when from a blank slate an image emerged. She laughed, seeing that naughty expression in Drusilla's eyes, which captured her personality. She had to admit that she had begun thinking of Drusilla as her own grandmother. She missed her grandmother, Renata, so much and in many ways Drusilla reminded her of her. Not so much how they looked but their indomitable spirits. She supposed that with age came wisdom.

It was getting dark outside when she began cleaning up after herself, sealing the tubes of oil paint, washing the brushes and removing the drop cloth from the floor.

After a soak in the tub she dried off and rubbed lotion into her skin. Completely nude, she stood in front of the full-length mirror. Her brown skin was mostly unscarred except for an inch-long scar on her right knee from when she was seven and fell from a tree she'd climbed in spite of being told not to by her parents. Her best friend at that time had been a boy named Pietro and he had loved climbing trees. She might not have defied her parents if he hadn't accused her of being afraid of heights. She had to prove she wasn't. Unfortunately, she got dizzy after climbing thirty feet into the tree and wound up losing her balance. The lush lawn had cushioned her fall for the most part, except for the knee which sustained a deep gash.

She carefully regarded her body in the mirror. She

was neither obsessed with perfection nor too critical of herself. Her body was strong and healthy. That mattered most to her. Not that that attitude hadn't been hard won. She'd gone through a period when she was self-conscious about her body. Many models who were always being judged by how much they weighed, and were stripped naked in front of designers, dressers and myriad other people in the fashion business, had to distance themselves from rude comments. If you were smart you began to take all snide remarks for what they were: thoughtless and petty. Her brown, long-limbed, fit body with its pert breasts and nicely rounded bottom would pass muster.

Her cell phone rang a little after seven. Eric said, "Are you dressed yet?"

Ana knew what that meant: he was taking the Harley for a spin tonight. She looked down at her slinky red dress. "No, I'm still trying to decide what to wear."

"How would you like to go to Mario's in Queens tonight? We love the place and there's room to park the bike on the street."

"Sounds like a plan," Ana said cheerfully. She didn't feel much like wearing heels tonight anyway.

"See you in twenty," said Erik, his voice husky.

Ana hung up the phone and went to her walk-in closet and began putting together an outfit conducive to a bike ride through the city.

She emerged ten minutes later wearing black jeans, black leather boots, and a red cashmere sweater. Just because she was going to be on the back of a Harley didn't mean she couldn't feel girly.

She'd checked the weather forecast earlier and it was going to be in the forties tonight. She chose a jacket with a warm lining and a knit cap to go over her simple braid down her back. A spray of her favorite perfume, which she walked through while it was still a mist in the air finished her preparations for tonight.

Erik was there on time, and when she opened the door her breath caught in her throat. He looked good in a suit, but he absolutely made her melt when he wore leather. His muscular body was made for jeans and biker boots. His black leather jacket was open and she couldn't help running her hand inside it to caress his pectorals through his soft denim shirt. Erik grasped her hand, pulled her against him, their pelvises touching. He gently reached up to smooth her brow with the pad of his thumb, and then he kissed her upturned mouth. His scent, the warmth of his mouth, the hard muscles beneath his hot skin all became temptations that Ana could not resist. She gave herself over to his kiss, completely abandoning any thoughts of decorum and what impression she might be making. She was hungry for him and enjoyed every erotic thrust of his tongue as he slowly tasted her. She relished the feel of his firm lips as he turned this way and that, maximizing her pleasure.

She gazed dreamily at him when they parted. Momentarily weak with desire, she smiled up at him. "You can't imagine how much I've missed you since this afternoon."

Erik laughed softly. "Yes, I think I can."

Ana grinned from ear to ear when she felt his erection on her thigh. "I think you do."

There was definitely something to the term lovesick, Erik thought. Only hours since he'd seen Ana and he could hardly wait to see her again, touch her again, feel her lips on his. Love was a kind of madness you never wanted to be cured of.

He grabbed her hand. "Ready?"

Over dinner Erik told her about Drusilla's accident and that she was just fine, no need to worry. Then he told her he'd mentioned to his dad that they were dating.

"How did he react?" she asked cautiously. She knew his family liked her and she liked them, but still she wanted their blessing.

Erik's golden-brown eyes held amusement in their depths. "Dad thought we were already secret lovers and Drusilla is just happy we've finally made it official."

"Your dad thought we were sleeping together?" Ana said, laughing nervously. "That surprises me."

"Me, too," Erik told her, "but I shouldn't have been. He's my father. He knew how I felt about you and he was maintaining a positive attitude about our relationship. Hoping we were more than friends even when we weren't."

"When you put it that way, it was sweet of him to think we were lovers," Ana said.

"It's a sign of how much he likes you," Erik said, his tone gentle. "They all do."

"I love them," Ana said simply.

Erik grasped her hand across the tiny table for two. Mario's, an elegant family-owned restaurant, had been a mainstay in its Queens neighborhood for more than fifty years. Sunday night was popular for couples and the restaurant was fully booked.

Each time Erik brought Ana here he thought it would be the ideal place to propose. The idea ran through his mind tonight, too, but he stamped it down, way down. It was much too soon for that. But he enjoyed entertaining the idea.

Mario's menu consisted of dishes from southern Italy, rich red sauces, handmade pastas, crisp vegetables, all cooked with slow deliberation.

He watched as Ana ate a forkful of pasta dripping in tomato sauce. She took a sip of red wine afterward and mopped up the remaining sauce on her plate with a piece of crusty bread. Bringing the bread to her lips she ate it with something akin to ecstasy in her expression. Erik smiled. "Enjoying your pasta?"

Ana looked down at her clean plate, "Enjoyed it."

They ordered two desserts and shared them. Erik fed her some of his lemon tart. She plied him with tiramisu. They took a walk after leaving the restaurant. The night was quiet on this street. Other couples were out, too, holding hands, sitting on benches or frequenting the open shops. Erik and Ana stopped to check out the display in a bookstore window.

"They've got the new Walter Mosley," said Erik. "I

know you'd love to get your hands on that. Too bad they're closed."

Ana peered at the book a pout forming, "It's a Leonid McGill mystery, too. I love that character."

Erik took her hand as they resumed their walk they put their arms about each other's waists and Ana put her head on his shoulder.

"This is what I love about New York," Erik said. "Even if what you want is a quiet evening out with your girl, you can find it somewhere in the five boroughs."

"I like Queens," Ana agreed. "There's much more greenery here. Houses actually have gardens."

Erik smiled at her use of gardens. Not many people he knew called a yard a "garden."

But Ana had grown up in Europe where people said this even if they didn't grow flowers or vegetables.

"Gardens aren't unheard of in Manhattan," he said. "I've seen some elaborate rooftop gardens."

"Yes, I suppose if you have the money you can have a garden put on your roof or your terrace," she conceded. "But I like these gardens better."

Erik stopped in his tracks and peered down at her. "We could put a garden on the terrace of the penthouse. There's plenty of room for one."

Erik lived in the penthouse of the building that Whitaker Enterprises owned in Manhattan. His father used to live there but had taken up permanent residence in Connecticut since his retirement. "In fact, there are a couple of vacancies in the building. Why don't you move in?"

He wanted to take back what he'd said the moment the words were out of his mouth. Ana would think he was moving way too fast. He had to slow himself down. But his first instinct was to take their relationship to the level where it should rightly be by now: totally committed.

She laughed softly instead. "Your dad thought we were lovers just because we spent so much time together as friends. Imagine what our families would think if we lived in the same building?"

"I'm sorry. I'm getting ahead of myself. On the other hand, we're consenting adults. What does it matter what they think?"

"My dad's a devout Catholic. Believe me, I've had enough preaching about remaining pure from him and my grandmother when I was growing up. It's a wonder I'm capable of a normal sex life. He laid into Dominic when Dominic started living with Elle and told him to marry her if he loved her, and stop stringing her along. Now, if you don't want a visit from my father, we should live in separate buildings for a while longer."

Chuckling, Erik said, "Fine. But I'm still going to have a garden planted for you."

"It's nearly November. It's too cold for a garden," Ana said.

"A greenhouse, then," he said. "You can grow flowers year round."

She squeezed him affectionately. "That's so romantic."

Erik hugged her close and kissed her cheek. "I'm going to enjoy spoiling you."

One of the things Erik had missed when they weren't dating was not being able to give Ana romantic gifts. He'd tried to give her a diamond bracelet for her birthday last year and she'd handed it back to him with, "You're so good to me, Erik, but this is not the sort of gift a friend gives a friend." It had been yet another reminder for him to keep his distance. He couldn't help resenting the moment just a little bit.

On the ride back to her loft, Ana clung to Erik, the side of her face pressed to his solid back. She was giddy with anticipation. Would tonight be the night? She had tried not to make herself nervous with wondering exactly when they would make love. Erik had said it had to be an event. What constituted an event to him, she wondered. As far as she was concerned, tonight's date had been eventful enough. In fact, hadn't their confession of love for each other been one?

At her building they ran up the stairs to the top floor. She paused at the door after unlocking it. It was Sunday night and it would only be polite to ask him if he wanted to come in for coffee, not being too insistent about it. He had work in the morning, after all. She didn't want to seem too eager. Going through the niceties would offset that notion.

Looking into his eyes, her own expression innocent, she softly said, "I've got a new Kona blend I'd like you to try."

"I'm game," said Erik and reached out and turned

the doorknob. Ana smiled seductively, her confidence shooting up instantly, as she backed inside, pulling him with her. She closed and locked the door then took his coat and put it in the foyer closet along with hers. Gesturing to the comfortable sectional in the living room area of the loft, she said, "Relax," knowing that word was a foreign concept to Erik.

She went to the kitchen. Erik went over to the far wall where her entertainment system was shelved. He put Adele's latest CD in the player. Although Ana was lately into classic blues performers she also liked contemporary artists if their sound harkened back to yesteryear.

In the kitchen Ana heard Adele's soulful voice. She smiled as she measured coffee beans into the grinder. Maybe he *was* going to make this an eventful night. She was getting excited by the prospect.

Once she'd gotten the coffeemaker going, she went back to see what Erik was up to. She found him in her studio looking at the portrait of Drusilla.

Hearing her footsteps on the hardwood floor he smiled at her. "You really are talented." He gazed at her with a mixture of awe and admiration, his expression so intense that Ana had to lower her own. She looked at the portrait instead. In it Drusilla was sitting in the garden at the New Haven house. It was springtime and she was surrounded by flowering trees and plants in huge clay pots.

"Don't mention it to her. It's her birthday gift."

Erik went to stand beside her as he continued admiring the painting. "She's gonna love it. However, I have to say you made her much more angelic-looking than she is in real life."

"That's how I see her," Ana said. She laughed shortly. "I'm fully aware her behavior frustrates you sometimes. She's headstrong, and says whatever comes to her mind. In that way she reminds me of Grandma Renata. But she's been sweet to me from the first time we met."

"It's true," said Erik. "She only tries to control family members." *Wait until we're married,* he thought. *She'll be on your case every day asking when you're going to make her a great-grandmother.*

"What was that?" said Ana, "You had the funniest expression on your face." She gazed up at him, brows raised inquisitively. "What were you thinking?"

He couldn't dare tell her what he'd been thinking. So he said, "I was just thinking how nervous I am being here alone with you when we've been alone countless times before."

That was true. Now that the dynamics had changed and there was actually the possibility of their making love tonight, he was nervous. He worried that if he made a move on her she would have the image of Jack Russo in the back of her mind. *Was she entirely over that creep?*

"I know," Ana said. "I'm nervous too and I've been tormenting myself trying to figure out what exactly you think an event is."

Erik laughed shortly and took her in his arms. "I

wish I'd never said that. It took some of the spontaneity out of what's happening between us. But I wanted you to know that getting you into bed is not my main goal. Marriage is. And if you want to wait until we're married, I would be willing to do that."

"Are you asking me to marry you?" She stared at him with wide eyes and an even wider grin.

"Honestly, I would have married you two years ago," Erik said. So there, the secret was out.

Ana was waiting for him to say the words, *Will you marry me,* or something to that effect. She blinked. "You were saying?" she gently prodded him.

Erik gave her a puzzled look. Then, it dawned on him what she was asking him and he decided to go the old-fashioned route. He got down on one knee right there in her studio and grasped her hand in his. "Ana Maria Corelli, will you do me the honor of becoming my wife?"

Tears sprang to Ana's eyes. "Yes, Jonathan Erik Whitaker, it would make me very happy to become your wife!"

Erik rose, and Ana flew into his arms. Then they were kissing hungrily with words of love interspersed between the kisses.

"I love you so much," he breathed.

"It's always been you," she told him. "How could I have been so blind?"

"I should have had the ring before I asked you."

"The ring doesn't matter. Just that you love me."

"My darling, you *will* get a ring!" Erik promised.

"Make love to me," said Ana breathlessly, her beautiful brown eyes beseeching him. Erik could not deny her a thing when she looked at him that way. However, as his feverish mind soon realized, there was a problem. He was not the sort of man who carried a spare condom in his wallet thereby making that telltale indentation in the leather. He was now looking at *Ana* beseechingly. "I didn't bring any condoms."

From the expression on Ana's face, a look of utter disappointment, he could tell she didn't have any, either. "I could go to an all-night drugstore."

Ana knew her neighborhood better than he did. "The closest drugstore closed at midnight."

That took the edge off their excitement. They gazed into each other's eyes and burst out laughing. "Are we lame, or what?" Erik said between guffaws. "Both of us undoubtedly with sex on our minds but neither of us thought to buy condoms. Is there any hope for us?"

"Obviously, not tonight," Ana quipped, "Ah, well, I've waited this long for you. I can wait another twenty-four hours. But you will be mine tomorrow night, do you hear me?" she asked sternly, the smile wiped entirely off her face. "I've got some serious pent-up sexual tension in need of release."

"Damn it, I'll get on my bike and ride until I find an open drugstore," Erik said, turning to head to the foyer closet where his keys were in his jacket pocket.

Ana grasped his arm. "You are not going out into the night when you can be here cuddling with your fiancée."

Erik looked into her upturned face and sighed in frustration. "I will never be caught unprepared again," he vowed.

Chapter 5

Ana stayed busy on Monday. She had an appointment to meet with Damon Cohen at his gallery to discuss the upcoming show. Scheduled for the first week of December, Damon assured her that her work was in competent hands.

When she arrived at the gallery in Soho, Damon was with a client. His receptionist, a tall thin redhead, her hair tucked away in a smooth chignon, smiled up at her and said, "Mr. Cohen is expecting you, Ms. Corelli. He won't be long. May I offer you a coffee while you wait?"

Ana rarely refused coffee, but she was very discriminating about where her coffee came from. "What kind?"

"It's Jamaican," said the receptionist.

"I'd love some, thank you," Ana replied pleasantly

as she sat on the off-white leather couch and crossed her legs.

The receptionist was back in less than a minute with a steaming cup of coffee complete with saucer and spoon. "Black, two sugars," she said, letting Ana know she remembered how she took her coffee.

"How thoughtful," said Ana, as she accepted the coffee and took a sip. "Delicious."

The receptionist smiled her appreciation and returned to her desk.

Ana enjoyed her coffee in contemplative silence. She wondered what Erik was doing right now? He was probably in a meeting. He conducted meetings via computer with the officers of the company from all over the world. He liked being abreast of any new developments, no matter how minor. It amazed her that he was capable of mentally juggling everything with such ease. But he said it was a talent he'd learned from his father who was famous for multitasking. Sometimes she thought his penchant for business was hereditary. He didn't mind working long hours, actually thrived on it.

Ana remembered all of the social events she'd invited him to that Erik had to miss because of work. As his friend, she'd been magnanimous and not complained. She vowed to be just as understanding now that they were engaged. Engaged! She still hadn't been able to convince herself this was really happening. Smiling, she finished her coffee and set the cup and saucer on the table in front of her.

"Ana!"

She looked up into the dark brown eyes of Damon Cohen. He was moving toward her, hand outstretched, with a huge grin on his good-looking face. In his late thirties, Damon was about her height with a deep tan and curly black hair that he wore shorn close to his well-shaped head. He wore glasses with black frames, which gave him an intelligent, although somewhat myopic look.

She put her hand in his and he pulled her to her feet straight into his arms for a warm hug. "You look wonderful," he said effusively. He peered at her, noting the glowing skin with very little makeup and how bright her dark eyes were. "What's happened to you since I saw you last?" he asked suspiciously.

Ana laughed softly as they made their way to his office, "I don't know what you mean," she said coyly.

"I expected you to come in looking drained. Weeks in your studio, working like a madwoman. I'm used to artists who suffer for their work. You look like you just spent a week on the beach in the Mediterranean."

"Actually, I went to Connecticut for the weekend," she said.

"Ah, with Erik," he said knowingly. "No wonder you look so good."

She and Damon had been friends since they met at a party a male model friend of hers threw at his gallery. The party was to launch the model's new fragrance and Damon's gallery was chosen as the venue for its chic, modern style. Once Ana admitted to him that she painted, he insisted on seeing her work and after seeing it he had pestered her to let him introduce her to the New York City art world. It was finally happening.

Damon had also insisted, upon meeting Erik, that Erik was in love with her and she would be a fool not to act on it. Ana had laughed it off.

Now, she was pleased to be able to shock and delight him with, "Erik asked me to marry him."

Damon screamed like a little girl. The receptionist, who was the only other person in the gallery since his client had left, shot up from her desk and looked in their direction with her mouth open in astonishment. She undoubtedly had never heard her employer make that sound before. "Are you all right?" she asked.

Damon waved her off with, "Fine, fine, sorry about that—as you were."

He briskly pulled Ana into his glass-enclosed office and closed the door. He hugged her again, and Ana could tell it was all he could do to resist jumping up and down.

Holding her at arm's length, he beamed. "I couldn't be happier for you, darling. I knew it would happen sooner or later. When's the wedding?"

He gestured to the mocha-colored designer couch. After they were seated he turned to her, his eyes riveted on her. "Or have you had the chance to plan yet?"

"No plans," Ana told him. "It hasn't been twenty-four hours since he asked. I probably shouldn't even be talking about it, but it's hard to hold it in. Sophia phoned earlier and I blurted it out. After she stopped laughing, she said exactly what you just said. It was only a matter of time."

"What was she laughing about?" asked Damon. He always loved a good humorous story. But Ana couldn't divulge what Sophia had found so funny.

It did replay in her mind, though.

She was barely out of bed before the phone rang and her sister was on the other end. "Matty won't let me sleep anyway so I decided to call you and see how your date went last night," Sophia said, curiosity clearly evident in her tone. "I can't believe this is your first date with Erik!"

Ana told her about dinner and the walk, and riding on the back of Erik's Harley. How sensual the whole night had been, culminating in their expression of love for each other and…she gave a dramatic pause…then he'd proposed.

"Oh, my God!" Sophia had yelled into Ana's ear. "He proposed after one date? That man is not wasting time. I knew I liked him for a reason. Then, I suppose, you took him to bed. I'm not trying to be nosy or anything, you don't have to answer if it isn't something you want to talk about, but I'm curious. I mean it's been nearly two years that you two have known each other and have kept your hands to yourselves. There must have been a lot of…um…tension to get rid of."

"Well, yeah," Ana said. "There was…is…a lot of tension."

"Is?" asked Sophia. "You mean you didn't do anything?"

"Neither of us were equipped for sex last night," Ana admitted sheepishly.

"You mean you didn't have any condoms?" her big sister asked, giggling loudly.

"Not one," Ana confirmed.

"That's unbelievable," Sophia said, laughing even louder. "It's been so long since either of you made love that neither of you thought to buy condoms? Can I call Mom and tell her, can I, please?"

"You'd better not tell anyone," Ana warned fiercely.

"I've gotta tell someone," Sophia insisted. "Matty, did you hear how totally clueless your auntie and soon-to-be uncle are?"

Ana laughed in spite of being irritated with her sister. "Let Matty be the only person you tell!"

"Okay, okay," Sophia agreed. "Then tonight is the night?"

"Definitely," Ana said with a sigh.

"Are you ready?" her nosy sister wanted to know.

"More than ready," Ana said right away.

"Yeah, I'm sure you are. What I meant was are you ready for how it's going to change your relationship with Erik?"

"Why would our relationship change?"

"Sweetie, sex changes everything. Even the most enlightened male will become an alpha male on you. If he even detects some other guy sniffing after you, he becomes a beast. It's the pheromones or something. Sex changes everything, I'm telling you. So be prepared little sister."

Ana laughed, "Come on, Erik is the sweetest, most understanding man I've ever met. Sex isn't going to turn him into a Neanderthal."

"It's a physical thing," Sophia insisted. "Love combined with sex turns men into protective, possessive, obsessive beasts. I ought to know, I'm married to one. Just like our mother and our grandmother before her. Ask Mom, she'll tell you."

"I am not phoning Mom with a question like that," Ana adamantly refused.

"Okay, don't say I didn't warn you," Sophia said lightly. Lowering her voice, she added, "I can't believe your nephew has fallen asleep, as loud as I was talking. I'm gonna put him to bed. Good night, sis, have fun tonight."

It was already morning in New York City, but Ana said, "Goodnight, sis," anyway.

Now, Ana smiled at Damon and said, "It was just something I said that struck her as funny."

"Well, I'm seriously thrilled," said Damon. "I love weddings. I can give you the number of my wedding planner if you like."

Damon had married his long-time partner, Sidney, last year. Ana had been one of the bridesmaids. It had been a simple, tasteful affair at the Waldorf Astoria, if you can have a simple affair at the world-famous luxury hotel.

"I'd like that," Ana said thankfully. It was good she had friends who were happy to advise her. She was sure her mother also was going to want to be in on the planning. Natalie Corelli had taken great pains to give Sophia the wedding of her dreams when she had married Matteo. And that had been a rushed affair since Sophia was expecting before the wedding. Natalie warned her that even though she adored Matteo and their child-to-be, she would not ultimately be pleased with wedding photos of her with a huge belly.

Damon got up to find the wedding planner's number. When he located it on his computer, he scribbled the name and number for Ana on a notepad. He went back and sat down beside her, offering her the sheet of paper.

"I suppose we should talk business, even though I could spend a delightful morning talking weddings." He paused and breathed deeply. "The first thing I decide on when I'm introducing a new artist is the theme. You are a portrait painter. Your work is so realistic it's startling. When someone stands before your work, studying it, absorbing the emotions you convey they can't help feeling transported. They know they're not in Kansas anymore, so to speak. So your theme is going to be *The Wizard of Oz*. You do know that story, don't you? You grew up in Italy. You might not be familiar with it."

"Oh, yes, I've seen the movie several times," Ana told him. "I love it."

"Very good," said Damon. "Well, in the beginning the movie is in black and white. Then, when Dorothy is transported to Oz, the movie is in color. Your show will begin with your drawings in charcoal and will progress to your larger, more colorful works. In my opinion, even

though you use real models in your work, finished results have a fantasy element to them."

Ana had been nodding in agreement. "I like the concept," she said.

"We will even have a yellow-brick road the night
of the show," Damon said, smiling. "I know people in
the theater who can make it happen. The patrons will
walk the yellow-brick road while they get the full effect of your work."

Ana looked at him in amazement, "No wonder you're
so successful," she exclaimed.

Damon smiled warmly. "I do know how to put on a
show. But, darling, you're going to be the star."

Ana's phone rang while she was headed back home
in a cab half an hour later. Seeing Erik's name and number in the display, she cooed, "Hello, how has your day
been going?"

Erik sighed deeply. She could tell by the tone of that
sigh that he missed her as much as she missed him. "I
can't think of anything except seeing you again."

She laughed huskily. "I'm suffering, too."

"Where are you?"

She told him.

"Can you come to my office at noon?"

"Sure," she immediately said, excitement coursing
through her.

"See you then," Erik said with a note of laughter in
his voice.

They said goodbye, and she relaxed in the back of the cab.

Her mind was running ahead of her, wondering what he was planning. Surely not making love in his office? The door *did* have a lock on it. She laughed softly to herself, wondering when she'd started entertaining sexy thoughts like that.

When she got there Abigail Sinclair, Erik's long-time secretary, a petite African-American woman in her mid-fifties, smiled at her and said with warmth, "Ana, it's lovely to see you. How are you, dear?"

"Great, Abby, and you?" said Ana, returning her smile.

"I'm well, thank you. Go right in, Erik's waiting."

Abby was one of Ana's favorite people. Married, with two grown children, she loved her job and she and her schoolteacher husband, Harry, doted on one another. Ana had observed them at several Whitaker Enterprises social events such as their annual Christmas party. Abby was invariably impeccably dressed in business suits and two-inch-heeled pumps, her long auburn hair in a bun, glasses either perched on the end of her nose or hanging on a magnetic clip on her chest. Abby was always solicitous but there was an added excitement in her hazel eyes today.

After Ana had been ushered into Erik's office, she knew why. A representative from Tiffany's was in Erik's office. Two armed guards stood over by the window trying to look inconspicuous. But they all turned to look at Ana when she walked into the room.

The woman from Tiffany's was in her sixties with wavy white hair that she wore in a pixie cut. She had bright blue eyes and when she smiled she revealed slightly crooked but white teeth. To Ana the fact that she hadn't gone to the trouble of having her teeth made perfect-looking spoke to her belief that she didn't need artifice to feel beautiful about herself. Ana liked that.

Erik smiled and met her halfway. "Sweetheart, I hope you don't mind. With both of us pressured with business obligations I thought it would be more convenient if Tiffany's came to us." Taking her hand, he led her over to his desk where the Tiffany's representative had spread a black velvet cloth and placed several engagement rings in their boxes upon it.

Ana was sure her face reflected her surprise but could not for the life of her fix her facial muscles to look any other way. "They're all beautiful," she said, her gaze taking in all of the diamonds. The quality of the stones was irrefutable. White diamonds expertly cut and polished. All of them were five carats or higher. Her eyes were not drawn to the large stones, though, but the beauty of the cut and how well the stones caught the light.

"Darling, this is Carol Richards. Ms. Richards, my fiancée, Ana Corelli."

The two women shook hands and Carol said, "It's wonderful to meet you, Ms. Corelli."

"Likewise," Ana said, smiling. She looked up at Erik. He smiled, his love for her evident in his golden-brown depths. "I was going to choose one myself, but

I thought it would be best to get your input." He gestured to the rings. "What do you think? Does one strike your fancy?"

Once again, Ana perused the rings. Square-shaped, pear-shaped, they were all beautiful, but the one that she liked the most was a five-carat solitaire in a platinum setting. She pointed to it.

Carol picked up the ring and slipped it onto her finger. It fit perfectly. Ana gazed down at it, turning it this way and that, marveling at how the stone caught the light and the many colors that sparkled inside it.

"How did you know which size to get?" she asked Erik.

"I just described you to Carol," he said.

"After years of experience, I'm a good guesser," said Carol modestly.

"I don't believe I'm saying this," Erik joked, "but you chose the smallest ring. It's okay to choose something larger, sweetheart. I don't like to brag, but I can afford it."

"This is perfect," Ana said. She raised to her tiptoes and kissed his cheek. "Thank you. I assure you this is the one for me."

"Actually," said Carol authoritatively. "Ms. Corelli has a good eye for diamonds. The ring she chose might not be the largest, but it is the highest quality of them all. Pure white and although it's nearly impossible to find a diamond without any faults whatsoever because they are a product of nature this comes close."

Erik kissed Ana's cheek. "And I thought you were being thrifty."

Everyone laughed.

"Very well," Erik said to Carol. "We'll take this one."

Carol smiled, her eyes twinkling as she looked at Ana, then Erik. "Congratulations on your upcoming nuptials. I hope you two will be very happy."

She shook hands with Erik, then Ana, after which she began packing up the remaining diamonds while Erik pulled Ana aside and hugged her tightly. "Now, if you should change your mind, you can always take it back."

Ana looked at him as if he'd lost his mind. "Exchange it? No, never. This ring will not leave my finger, ever." Then, they kissed.

It took Carol clearing her throat to tear them apart. "If you'll sign here," she said to Erik. Erik went over and quickly signed the form. He glanced at the final sales price and didn't even flinch. "Thank you, Carol."

"It was my pleasure," said Carol who promptly signaled to the guards that it was time to depart. One of them opened the door for her and preceded her. The other followed.

When they were alone, Ana threw her arms around Erik's neck in excitement. "You're so sneaky. I thought you wanted me to come by for…"

"Love in the afternoon?" he guessed, his eyes alight with humor.

"Yes!" Ana admitted almost defiantly. At the time

it had sounded like a good idea to her. "Don't tell me it never crossed your mind."

Erik laughed softly and smoothed her brow with the pad of his thumb, a gesture he was fond of doing, Ana recalled, just before he kissed her, which he did, long and passionately. When they came up for air, he said, "I couldn't make love to you with Abby right outside my door. I'd never be able to look her in the eyes again."

Ana left Erik's office feeling as though she were floating on a cloud of happiness. And when she got home, she saw that someone had left a package at her door. Once she was inside she opened it. It was the Walter Mosley book she had admired in the bookstore window the night before.

Chapter 6

Etta James belted out lyrics to "I Just Wanna Make Love to You" as Ana danced around the living room area of the loft, supposedly cleaning. She wasn't the neatest person in the world. When they were teens her sister, Sophia, used to say her bedroom looked like a tornado had hit it. Once she was living on her own, however, Ana had learned to pick up after herself. Now her house looked shabby chic. At least that's how she liked to think of the juxtaposition of ultra-modern furnishings with antiques thrown in here and there. And the kitchen had recently had an upgrade. Now all the appliances were stainless steel, the countertops granite, and the floor Italian tile. Except for the two bathrooms, which had tile floors, the remainder of the loft had hardwood floors.

Ana warbled along with the CD.

She'd been listening to Etta ever since she'd returned from Erik's office. She would clean a little, dance a little and admire her ring—a lot. She couldn't stop smiling, sometimes laughing out loud. She was glad she was alone because anyone observing her would think she was certifiably insane. She wanted to talk with someone, but she had already tried to phone her mother and the message service had come on and she had not wanted to leave a mere message about this momentous occasion. This news had to be told live, not recorded. The same thing had happened when she'd phoned Sophia. She couldn't talk to anyone in Erik's family because he wanted to tell them about their engagement when they got together in New Haven for Thanksgiving. That was nearly a month away.

Finished dusting and straightening up in the living room, she moved on to the kitchen.

On the way home she'd stopped by the market and bought fresh salmon and salad fixings. She was making one of Erik's favorite meals tonight: grilled salmon with spicy red pepper sauce, a baked potato and garden salad. It was simple to prepare yet delicious and light. She didn't want anything weighing them down tonight. Nothing was going to go wrong when things started getting heated between them.

It had crossed her mind to go to a spa and get the works: hair, nails, facial, wax. But she was plucked and prodded enough in her work. Erik liked her natural. She liked her natural state, as well. Besides, doing all that bordered on the obsessive and she was already neurotic enough. She kept her legs and underarms shaved, took long baths, after which she moisturized. That was sufficient.

Erik was coming at eight. By seven, she had the salmon ready to put on the grill, the salad and the pepper sauce were prepared and the potatoes washed and ready to pop into the microwave and then afterward put on the grill a few minutes to make the skins crisp. A trick her dad had taught her via one of their Skype cooking lessons. He was the chef in the family. Her mother could cook but didn't really enjoy it. Carlo relished cooking all the recipes his mother, Renata, had taught him. Because Ana hadn't paid much attention when he'd tried to teach her to cook while she was growing up, she had persuaded him a couple years ago to teach her over the computer. So about once a month, they got together via Skype and he taught her another recipe from his ever-expanding handwritten cookbook. She was a quick learner and was becoming quite proficient in the kitchen.

She was just thinking she should start getting ready for her date when her cell phone rang. A quick glance at the display told her it was her mother phoning.

"Mom!" she answered with a huge grin. "Where have you been? I've been trying to get in touch."

"I know, I know, sweetie," said Natalie a bit breathlessly. "I saw all the missed calls. What's up? You sound good. You're not sick or anything?"

Ana laughed shortly. "No, I'm fine. Well, not fine,

exactly. I'm excited, a little scared, maybe. I mean this is such a huge step to take. It's something I only want to do once, like you and Daddy…"

"Ana Maria Corelli," Natalie interrupted her, her tone frustrated. "What are you talking about?"

Ana sighed, still grinning. "Erik asked me to marry him."

"Oh, my God. Carlo, get in here—your baby girl's engaged!" Natalie yelled, laughter bubbling up. Then, Ana could hear her mother talking to her father in the background.

"Erik finally popped the question! Okay, here, but I want to speak back with her when you're done," Natalie's voice trailed off as she handed the phone to Carlo.

Her father came on the line. "Is this true, *bambina?* You have accepted his proposal?"

"Yes," Ana told her father, her voice confident. "I love him, Daddy."

Carlo gave a resigned sigh. "Well, I suppose, your mother and I have a new son-in-law."

"You don't sound too happy about it," Ana said with a laugh to conceal the hurt. She had expected her father to sound as excited as her mother about her upcoming nuptials.

Her mother must have snatched the phone from her father's hand because hers was the next voice Ana heard, and she sounded miffed. "Honey, don't pay any attention to your father. You're the last daughter he has to walk down the aisle and he doesn't think there's a man alive who's good enough for you. Erik is a good man. I like him, and your father will learn to like him, or else."

Ana smiled, and said, "Give Dad a kiss for me and tell him I'm sorry but I had to grow up sometime. I'd better get ready for my date with your future son-in-law now. Love you both."

"We love you, too, sweetie," Natalie assured her. "Give our best to Erik."

A quarter after seven, she started counting down the minutes. A soak in the tub helped her to relax. Taking pains to smooth scented lotion over every inch of her body and making sure her nails were done kept her mind focused. Otherwise, she kept thinking about the last time she'd made love to Jack Russo and how she had thought of it as an act of love only to find out it had been a farewell performance. The next day she'd gotten a text saying, "Sorry, babe, this isn't working out. I wish you much happiness in your future endeavors. Truly, I do." It had been the longest text message she'd ever gotten from him. She immediately phoned him. He didn't answer, of course. She left a message that was brief, to the point and only two words. After she'd verbally given him the middle finger, she felt better, but the feeling didn't last long because she'd made the mistake of giving him her heart, one of the most worthless human beings to walk the planet. How could she have been so idiotic? She questioned her common sense. She questioned her ability to tell a decent human being from an indecent one. Most of all she questioned her taste in men.

Tonight is going to be so much different from that other night, long ago she thought confidently.

She had done her penance, suffered through the indignity of making a fool of herself over a man who wasn't worthy of her. She had earned the right to happiness.

When the doorbell rang, she was dressed in a short black dress that clung to her curves, and a pair of sexy, black Ferragamo sandals. Her wavy black hair was parted in the middle and fell down her back. Her lips were red and pouty, and her dark eyes were smoldering.

She opened the door and Erik stood there with deep red roses in one hand and a bottle of wine in the other. She heard his sharp intake of breath and enjoyed the deliberate, sensual perusal of her body. Her efforts had been rewarded. "Wow," was all he said before stepping into the loft.

Ana was likewise delighted by his appearance. She made that perfectly clear by relieving him of the roses and the wine and setting both on the foyer table, then grasping him by his jacket's lapels and pulling him down for a lingering kiss. One of Erik's muscular arms went around her waist and held her tightly while the other caressed her back and slipped further down to squeeze her behind. He was hard in seconds, and softly groaned with pleasure against her mouth.

Ana molded her body to his. She inhaled his heady scent, masculine and clean. His touch made her core melt. Her nipples grew erect and pressed against the fabric of her bra magnifying her arousal. Her sex throbbed. She was ready, so ready.

She tore her mouth from his. She smiled seductively. "I made dinner for you."

"Smells wonderful," Erik returned, devouring her with his eyes. It was apparent that food was the last thing on his mind right now. "It'll keep, won't it?"

"Oh, yeah," she breathed, and once again their lips were locked in a passionate embrace. Erik picked her up. Ana wrapped her legs around him and he carried her to the bedroom.

Anticipating an eventful night, Ana had readied the bed, folding the comforter down to the foot of the bed, and turning back the top sheet. Erik gently set her down and began undressing her. He slowly unzipped her dress and pulled it off her shoulders. Ana let the dress fall in folds to the floor. She stood in a skimpy teddy whose color nearly matched her brown skin. Erik bent and planted kisses along the curve of her neck, enjoying the warmth and fragrance of her skin. His nerve endings were on fire with pent-up desire. Touching her greatly enhanced his urgent need. He closed his eyes momentarily thinking that if he denied himself the sight of her it would ease the tension. He was wrong. Even if he were blind, her smell, the softness of her skin would drive him to distraction. Ana did not once think to close her eyes. She didn't want to miss a thing. She reveled in the fact that it was she he wanted so badly that…and she touched him to make sure…he was so hard he was about to burst! She felt the pulse in her neck where his lips were kissing right now throb with excitement. Her heart was racing.

Erik's hand gently squeezed her breast. She sighed with contentment. His hand slipped inside her bra and cupped her naked breast. That nearly made her scream with delight, but she muffled the exclamation and panted instead. Erik obviously took this as a sign to get a move on because after that he quickly dealt with the bra and pulled the teddy off her. She now stood before him in her bikini panties. Erik stared for a moment, unable to take his eyes off her. He had known she would be beautiful unclothed, that was a given, but anticipation paled in comparison to reality. Her breasts were firm, round and with nipples that looked so sweet, he had to taste them. When his tongue touched one of them he felt her tremble with pleasure, and a soft gasp escape from between her swollen lips.

He thought she might swoon. But he was wrong. She reached for his belt buckle. Her hand inadvertently touched his manhood and he steeled himself against coming too soon. He had to hastily back up, saying, "Let me." At this point he knew that their first time would not be slow and easy. They were both too excited for that.

While he got undressed, Ana peeled off her bikini panties with nary a blush in sight.

Now they were both naked and both got their fill of each other in all their glory. Ana's eyes rested on him and the smile on her lips told him she liked what she saw. Inspired by that smile, he reached for her and she went into his arms. Their mouths touched and he found himself kissing her almost shyly, feeling her out, then he felt her relent and give herself over to him. From that point on, their movements felt natural, as if this were not their first time at all, but one of many supremely intimate moments during which giving and taking of physical gratification was as natural as breathing.

He laid her on the bed and rained kisses all over her. His hands knew her every curve. With a great deal of joy he partook of her, her thighs wantonly spread open and with her writhing beneath him, until she moaned loudly and trembled in his arms. Then he got up and put on the condom. She watched him, could not take her eyes off him, and when he returned to the bed, she welcomed him inside of her and clung to him with renewed ardor. His thrusts were deep and satisfying to Ana. She held on to his butt, feeling the muscles contract with each push. After some time passed, she came. And it felt so good. At last, she knew what the difference was between making love to someone and just having sex. When you were in love the climax felt a hundred times better. It was sublime.

They lay looking in each other's eyes, smiling contentedly. Erik spoke first, "We're perfect together."

Ana, who felt full of emotions fighting for prominence inside of her, nodded. She hadn't known she would feel this way, full of joy that kept building in momentum until she feared she would burst into tears. She now wouldn't be plagued by her last encounter with

Jack Russo. Jack who? Sophia was right. Jack was a glitch in her sexual past. Erik was her future.

She reached up and gently touched his cheek. "How could it be anything less?"

"You really believe that?" Erik asked hopefully. She looked so beautiful to him, her hair wild and sexy, a faint layer of perspiration on her skin from making love. He could die a happy man right now. For so long he'd been in love with her, wishing that one day soon she would see that he was the man for her. Yes, she'd accepted his marriage proposal, but making love to her was an even bigger step in their relationship. It meant she trusted him with her heart. No matter what some guys say about their ability to make love to as many women as they can get in bed and walk away unaffected the next day, it was a lie. Oh, it affected you all right. Depending on your circumstances it either served to harden your heart or leave it vulnerable to being broken into pieces.

Peering deeply in his eyes, Ana smiled and softly said, "With all my heart. I can't regret how long it's taken us to get to this point, though, because the time we spent together as friends only strengthened my love and respect for you. I got to know the real you."

"Oh, yeah?" said Erik playfully, white teeth flashing in a grin. "Tell me three things you know about me, and I don't mean something simple like my favorite color is blue."

Ana pursed her lips, pretending this was an arduous task. "Hmm, let's see. When you were a boy of nine you stole your dad's car and went joyriding. This was in Connecticut. You probably would've gotten yourself killed in New York."

"Who told you that?" Erik asked genuinely surprised.

"Drusilla," Ana said, laughing. "She didn't swear me to secrecy so I think it's safe to divulge the name of my source."

"Okay, number two?"

"You have a copy of the *Sports Illustrated* that has me on the cover in your nightstand drawer."

"How long have you known that?" he asked, feeling not in the least guilty about being found out.

"Almost immediately after it hit the newsstands," she said. "I broke a nail while I was at your place and I couldn't find a nail clipper in your medicine cabinet so I figured you kept one in your nightstand drawer like I do."

"You didn't say anything," he said, his tone questioning.

"No, I didn't want to get into why you had it there. I knew we were attracted to each other. We have been from the beginning. But I was comfortable with what we had. I didn't want to risk losing it. You understand?"

"Of course," he said gently, and kissed her chin.

"Now that we can talk about it…you didn't do anything naughty with my *Sports Illustrated* cover, did you?"

Erik laughed shortly. "I take the fifth."

She giggled. "Don't be embarrassed. I had to invent ways of surviving without jumping you, too."

"Such as?" he asked, brows raised in an askance expression.

"The detachable showerhead in my shower got a work out," she admitted, blushing even if she *were* lying naked in bed with her lover.

"I'm shocked," Erik said, feigning horror. "Okay, on to number three."

"I know you never got over your mother leaving," Ana said seriously, which instantly killed the levity in the conversation.

For a moment Erik looked somewhat stricken. He was quiet for a full thirty seconds and those thirty seconds felt like hours to Ana who instinctively knew she had brought up an unwelcome subject.

Erik fought for the right words to say. He was not aware Ana had perceived how he felt about his mother. She had been there when Mari had suddenly reentered his and Belana's lives more than a year ago. Ana had held him after she had died. In fact, she had refused to let him spend the night alone and they had talked for hours before he'd fallen asleep, exhausted.

"I never said anything," he murmured, and sat up in bed. He busied himself by going into the bathroom and cleaning himself up.

Ana sat up in bed, too, and said, "You didn't have to say anything. It was written all over your face when you looked at her. I could feel waves of emotion coming off you whenever you talked about her before and after she died. Have you forgiven her?"

She could see into the bathroom from the bed. Erik thought about shutting the door to shut Ana out if only for a few moments. He needed privacy because he was not ready to discuss his mother. Or the impact her desertion had had on him, even if he claimed she had none at all.

Ana rose and went into the bathroom, too, which had a tub and a separate shower. "You don't have to answer that," she said, and went to turn on the hot water in the shower. "I'm going to take a quick shower. You're welcome to join me."

Erik relaxed and followed her into the stall, not saying a word. He didn't want their earlier rapport to end. He inwardly chided himself for his inability to be forthcoming about his mother. But then again he had no practice in the matter. For years he was stalwart and denied feeling anything about her. He thought the best defense was to pretend not to care. It was her loss if she didn't want anything to do with her son and daughter.

His father, the good man that he is, refused to badmouth Mari. He simply told Erik and Belana that Mari had made bad choices and someday she would realize her mistake.

Someday wound up being too late. By the time she had come to that conclusion she was dying of lung cancer. The few weeks she spent with him and Belana could never make up for years of neglect. Erik was a man, though, and saw to it that she had the best care possible.

And when she drew her last breath, he and Belana had been there to gently usher her out of this world. That's the least he thought he could do.

So why couldn't he talk about her with the woman he loved?

Ana ran her soapy hands across his broad shoulders as she stood in front of him in the shower. She didn't seem to mind getting her hair wet. It lay in ringlets about her lovely face. Her golden brown skin was beaded with drops of water. The contrast of her skin with those dark chocolate eyes killed him. He got weak with desire whenever she looked at him intently like she was now. He wanted to bare his soul, give her anything she wanted. "For a long time," he blurted out, "I thought I'd wind up just like my father—abandoned by the woman I loved. I know it makes no sense. I'm not my father. But children learn by example and my example was an extremely hardworking man who had been left by his beautiful wife for a poor man she lusted-after. I got the lusted after part from Drusilla when I got older and she stopped trying to hide the details from me. My mother, who was a ballet dancer, as you know, left my father for a handsome French dance instructor. She threw away her marriage and her two children for him."

Ana was afraid to interrupt. Sometimes you just had to be quiet and let the other person talk.

"Growing up I went through all kinds of emotions concerning Mari. Sometimes I hated her. Sometimes I missed her so much it hurt. Sometimes I prayed that she'd come back to us. When she did come back I felt cheated because she didn't have very much time left. Have I forgiven her? I realize that my forgiving her means nothing, she's gone, but, yeah, I guess I have forgiven her even though I sometimes still feel like that little lost boy inside. Because of her I was afraid of letting go and truly loving someone until you came along with your own neuroses." He smiled at her.

Ana laughed. "Yeah, me and my trust issues."

"You weren't the only one with issues. Loving you has freed me. I'm not afraid of being abandoned anymore."

"And I trust you," said Ana, smiling up at him.

"Good," said Erik, bending his head to claim her mouth in a searing kiss that left her weak in the knees. As he pulled her firmly against him Ana realized he'd recovered from their earlier session in bed and was ready to go again. She smiled against his hungry mouth. She fleetingly wondered if the shower floor were too slippery for them to make love right here. Erik's back was against the tiles. Now the shower's spray was hitting the back of Ana's body. She gazed up. "Do you think we could do it here?"

Erik shook his head in the negative. "No, baby, I'm not going to take a chance on you getting hurt."

Ana's stomach growled loud enough for both of them to hear.

"Besides, you're hungry," Erik said. "Come on, let's dry off. I'm a big boy, I can wait."

Ana looked pointedly at his erection, her expression doubtful. "Are you sure?"

"It'll calm down in a minute," Erik joked.

So they dried off, Ana put on her bathrobe, styled her damp hair in a hastily done braid down her back, and Erik slipped into his clothes of jeans and shirt. They went into the kitchen where Ana fired up the grill and put the prepared salmon and the potatoes on it while Erik set the table. They talked while they worked.

"Damon thinks the show is going to be a hit." She told him about her visit with Damon today. "I'm nervous."

"You have no need to be," Erik said with confidence. "You're brilliant."

"I'm an unknown entity," she said realistically. "The critics will tear me to shreds. A model trying to paint, they'll say? It's hilarious. That gossip show, I can't remember what it's called…"

"Anyway," Ana said as she adjusted the temperature on the grill, being mindful that fish cooked quickly, "they'll probably have people stationed outside the gallery getting opinions from people leaving the show and even if they like my work they'll have catty remarks for the viewing audience."

"You'll let it roll off your back," Erik said. "You've soldiered through bad reviews before."

"Yeah, but they didn't matter," Ana said. "I learned to detach my emotions from what people said about me."

"Same thing," Erik said. "You'll survive. We all have to take the knocks when we're doing something we love and are not going with the flow anymore. Independent thinkers are usually deemed nuts until everyone realizes they were on to something all along. At least you're doing what your heart desires. Imagine all the people out there who never took the risk. We could have had any number of inventors with wonderful ideas that never got off the launching pad. Writers who wrote great novels that never saw the light of day. Stick to your dreams."

"God, I love you!" Ana exclaimed, her eyes dancing with delight. She peeked at the salmon on the grill. "I think the fish is ready. But the potatoes need to stay on the grill a little longer so the skins will get crisp."

"She's beautiful and she cooks," said Erik.

"Well, she cooks some things," Ana said. "I'm slowly learning. I won't be writing a cookbook anytime soon."

"Then you'd say you're not a domestic goddess?" joked Erik.

"If it's a domestic goddess you want to marry, keep looking," Ana said truthfully. "I'm messy and, while I like to cook, I can prepare only around seven dishes with any hope of them turning out edible."

"Don't worry, darling, I can cook," Erik assured her.

"That's right, you can," said Ana as if the thought had just occurred to her. Erik had fed her numerous times. He wasn't a master chef, but he knew his way around a pasta dish and grilled a steak to perfection. And his pancakes were to die for. He'd learned his culinary skills from Drusilla whose belief was men needed to know how to feed themselves and not base their search for a mate on whether or not she could cook.

Women have to work nowadays just like men, Drusilla told him. And no matter how much money you have you should never have to depend on someone else preparing your meals.

"Your grandmother taught you well," she said. "I have to thank her next time I see her."

"Which will be on Thanksgiving," Erik reminded her.

"Yes, and I must remember not to wear my ring into the house because she'll spot it like a hawk on a mouse," Ana said, laughing.

"You've got that right," Erik agreed, imagining Drusilla's expression when they told her about the engagement. She would happily shout "Hallelujah!"

To be honest, he felt like shouting it himself.

Chapter 7

Like every holiday season, that period between Halloween and New Year's Eve, time seemed to speed up for Ana. The first week of November she had to fly to Tahiti to be filmed and photographed in a tropical setting for Dare's spring campaign. The perfume she represented in print and TV ads was selling quite well and there was talk of a whole line of complementary products to go with the perfume: shampoo, conditioner, skin lotion and bath salts. When she arrived for the shoot she thought someone would mention her weight gain but Josh Cannon, who worked for the cosmetics company and was coordinating the shoot, only said, "You look gorgeous, so full of life, what's your secret?"

Ana laughed and said, "I'm in love."

"That's better than cosmetic surgery," Josh avowed, laughing along with her.

Later that day Ana had cracked up when she was being poured into an ankle-length billowy white dress whose tight bodice produced prodigious cleavage and the wardrobe lady remarked, "Have you had a boob job since the last time I dressed you?"

"No, just a bit of happy weight," Ana told her.

Ana enjoyed the shoot. The weather was balmy compared to New York City's and she was spoiled between sessions with fresh fruit and spring water and the male model working with her had a repertoire of jokes that kept her laughing.

At the end of the shoot she got to see some of the film footage. Josh was right. She looked extremely happy and healthy. She and the male model appeared very much in love as they walked on the beach, shared a romantic dinner and stood wrapped in each other's arms as the breezes ruffled her dress and hair, the backdrop of the beach at night augmenting the sensual feel of the scene.

With the job done, she got the first flight back to New York. She arrived at JFK on a Saturday afternoon and was met at the terminal by Erik who picked her up in a bear hug as if he hadn't seen her in weeks instead of mere days.

Ana dropped her carry-on bags and hugged him tightly, breathing in his male essence as she did so, "I can't believe I've only been gone a few days. You were constantly on my mind."

Erik was too busy kissing her to answer her. And Ana forgot everything as they gave each other a proper hello. But they had to come up for air sometime and when they did, Erik said, "I think I must be addicted to you. No matter how busy I was I couldn't help remembering how you sound, how you smell, how you feel."

"You're so sweet," Ana said, reaching up to wipe the lipstick from his lower lip with the pad of her thumb. She was happy he'd missed her as much as she'd missed him. They picked up her bags and made their way across the terminal, talking all the way.

"How did it go?" he asked.

"It was great, everyone concentrated on their jobs. No drama. It was a dream shoot."

"Good," Erik said, his arm about her waist. Lucky for him Ana packed lightly for her frequent jaunts so he had a free arm to hug her with. The way she put it her employers provided her wardrobe, anyway. She needed to pack only the necessities.

"How was work for you?" she returned.

"Headaches," said Erik. "We're experiencing some suspicious losses at our dairy in Minnesota. I'm going to have to go check it out on Monday."

"Minnesota," Ana said glumly, "Where it's already probably below freezing this time of year?"

"You betcha," Erik joked with a passable Minnesotan accent.

Laughing, Ana said, "I'm not inviting myself along on this trip."

Erik squeezed her. "You mean you don't like biting

wind and snow? I was going to suggest a cabin in Aspen over the Christmas holidays."

"Just you and I?" asked Ana, her interest piqued.

"We don't need anyone else."

"That, I'm up for," Ana assured him.

"Then I'll reserve our cabin," Erik promised.

In the back of her mind Ana was thinking this would be the first time in years she hadn't gone home for Christmas. How would her parents take the news? She'd joked with Sophia about going someplace romantic with Erik, but that had only been wishful thinking.

They walked on in silence and when they got to the car Erik had hired so that he wouldn't have to go through the hassle of parking, he held the door open for her. Once the driver pulled away from the curb, he said, "Something on your mind?"

"I haven't missed Christmas in Milan since I moved here," she told him.

"Sweetheart, I'll understand if you want to go home for Christmas."

Ana looked deeply in his eyes. She saw only love and trust reflected back at her. Yes, he would make the sacrifice if it would make her happy.

"Would you go with me?"

"Sorry, I just couldn't spare the travel time," Erik said regrettably. "My work schedule won't allow it. Aspen I could do, but not Italy."

Yes, Ana thought sadly, going to Milan was not just a weekend getaway.

"I'll wait and go home in the New Year," she decided.

She would miss her family and all the accoutrements of Christmas with them provided. However, she and Erik were building a life together. Time and effort went into a good relationship.

He smiled. "I'm serious. I would understand."

"I know," she said softly. "But you work so hard. It would be great to get away for a couple days alone with you. Aspen, it is."

"All right," Erik conceded. However he still felt unsure about the situation.

On Monday after he'd boarded the company plane for Minnesota he put in a call to Abby. She answered in her usual efficient manner, "What can I do for you, Erik?"

"I have a dilemma," Erik said. "One that needs your special touch. Let me explain."

Five minutes later Erik could hear the smile in Abby's voice when she said, "I'd be happy to arrange everything. Consider it done."

"You're a godsend, Abby," said Erik with warmth. "I don't know what I'd do without you."

Abby had laughed softly. "Just make sure I get an invitation to the wedding."

"You and Harry will be there to dance the night away," Erik promised. "See you when I get back."

"Have a safe trip," Abby said and rang off.

Erik hung up the phone and relaxed in the plush leather seat. The flight attendant stopped next to him. "We're getting ready to take off, Mr. Whitaker. Please buckle your seat belt and turn off any electronic devices."

In Minneapolis, a hired car was waiting to take him to the nearby town where the plant manager and key members of his staff were waiting to meet with him. He enjoyed the scenery as the car sped toward the plant. Cows grazed in pastures. It was snowing but not heavily. He supposed it was still too early for one of Minnesota's snowstorms. But it was definitely cold outside at 28 degrees. And the wind was biting. He had checked the weather before the trip, though, so he was dressed warmly enough.

His cell phone rang and he took it out of his inside coat pocket and glanced at the display. It was his father, John. "Hey, Dad, what's up?"

"Just thought you should be advised that when I acquired the plant in Harris, Minnesota, the plant manager and the owner were at odds," he said. "I had both of them vetted and decided that if the owner sold, the manager could keep his job. Olsen is a good man. Hadn't had any trouble since then, till now. Harris is a small town and relatives of the former owner work at the plant. Maybe one of them holds a grudge."

"That's a possibility," said Erik. "We'll see." He already had a plan in the works.

Later, at the meeting, Jim Olsen, the plant manager appeared relieved to see Erik. He was a tall, heavyset man with blond hair and brows and a somewhat florid face. He introduced the other four persons seated around the conference room table. Then he and Erik sat down. "I'm sorry you had to come all this way," he began. "But the accountants were unable to pinpoint exactly why we've experienced losses in the last two quarters."

Jim had emailed Erik files with the most recent numbers. Erik noticed a ten percent drop in profits in the past nine months. His auditors found that the amount of stock ordered by stores remained high. However stores were reporting that they were not receiving the right amount of stock they had ordered. To Erik that meant someone was intercepting outgoing stock before it could be shipped to stores. In which case he had to discover who was doing it and get proof of their guilt. To that end, a week ago he had hired a local private detective to keep the loading dock under surveillance until further notice. He told this to the five people sitting at the conference table with him now. "I'm expecting the detective any minute," he informed them.

Erik wasn't sure his hunch was correct, but what his father had earlier told him made him somewhat confident that he was on the right track.

Jim Olsen's secretary stuck her head in the conference room. "Mr. Olsen, there is a Ms. Valerie Estes here to see you. She says she has important information for you."

His color turning even more florid, Jim hastily stood. "Show her in, Ms. Bern."

A tall brunette dressed in a dark pantsuit and a heavy coat entered the room carrying a black satchel. Erik noticed that when she set the bag on the conference table she did it with care. Jim made hasty introductions and once Erik had been identified, Ms. Estes gave him an almost imperceptible nod with a slight smile on her face. "I believe I have the information you requested, Mr. Whitaker," she said, her tone businesslike. From her satchel she retrieved a laptop, which she set on the conference table, opened and switched on. In only a couple of minutes she clicked on a file and opened it. "Please take a look at this," she said.

Everyone gathered around the laptop's screen and watched as a man approached the loading dock of the plant. It was early morning according to the time posted at the bottom of the screen. It was still dark out. He unlocked the loading-dock door and since it was the rolling kind, he pushed up on it and the mechanism did the rest. Then the viewing audience noticed a large van being backed up to the loading dock. Two other men got out and leaped onto the dock and followed the first man into the plant. Minutes later they returned with hand trucks loaded with boxes of the plant's dairy products.

"Do you recognize those men?" asked Erik of the five plant employees in the conference room. No one said a word, but Erik could tell they did. He sighed. It was time to clean house.

After a couple minutes, Jim spoke up. "I'm sorry to say one of them is my son, Jim, Jr. I don't know the names of the other two, although they look familiar."

"I do," said Bob Holstein, supervisor of the shipping department. "I hired them about a year ago." He looked regrettably at Jim. "Jim, Jr. recommended them."

Erik turned to Jim and placed a hand on his shoulder and squeezed reassuringly.

"Look, there is no easy way to do this, but I'll give you two options. You can fire Jim, Jr. and the other two men and have security cameras installed in the loading area. That was an oversight. Or we can let the police handle it. I'm truly sorry it turned out this way."

"So am I," Jim said with a hangdog expression. His fellow employees offered sympathy. Erik pulled the private detective aside. "Thank you for your assistance, Ms. Estes."

"Sometimes," she said with a glance in Jim Olsen's direction, "this job sucks."

Erik knew what she meant. He felt bad for Jim Olsen. However the situation had to be handled and the culprits punished.

When the conference room had been cleared of everyone except him and Jim Olsen, he looked at Jim with regret. "I realize at this point you don't think things can go back to how they were before this incident, but they can. My father tells me you're a good man, Jim. You run this plant well and you're fair with your employees. They obviously respect you. What's more, you seem to enjoy your job. Don't let this affect your satisfaction in it. I don't hold you responsible for what happened here." He held out his hand.

Jim gratefully shook it and said, "It's going to be hard. My wife will cry her heart out over the situation. Jim, Jr. has been in trouble before, and we thought he was trying to straighten his life out."

"I have every bit of confidence in you, Jim," Erik said sincerely.

Jim let go of his hand and walked over to the large window that looked down on the employee parking lot. "Twenty-five years in this job with a spotless record and it's come to this. I should have been watching him more closely when he moved back into the house. Of course, we couldn't let him be homeless. It really pisses me off that while I was sleeping he was stealing my keys to steal from the company." His eyes were tormented when he faced Erik again. "This is going to kill my wife. But I'm going to have to put him out, and let him fend for himself."

Erik didn't know what to say to that, not being a father himself. He had no sage advice to offer. Sometimes you had to make hard choices in life.

"That'll be tough," was all he said.

Jim nodded in agreement, then seemed to gather strength from someplace deep inside and said, "It has to be done."

Erik left the plant soon after that. The hired car drove him back to the airport in Minneapolis and the company plane was ready to take off within minutes. Erik had known the flight plan ahead of time and had made it back to the plane with minutes to spare.

As they winged their way back to New York, he slept, which is what he resorted to when he didn't want to think anymore. He honestly had not guessed that the culprit could have been someone so close to one of his employees. That kind of betrayal was difficult to get over. He wished Jim and his wife good luck.

He slept the entire flight and awakened only when the plane was touching down. It was dark in the city. The November air was chilly but nowhere near as cold as it had been in Minnesota.

He went directly to Ana's loft in Greenwich Village without having phoned ahead. It was around eight in the evening, and he wouldn't have been surprised if she were out. But he wanted desperately to see her.

He could use some comfort and when he needed comforting he automatically thought of Ana. The best part of his job was helping save people's jobs. The worst part was seeing someone emotionally devastated as Jim Olsen had been this afternoon.

She swung the door open and let out a scream of delight. She was in his arms in an instant and kissing him a second after that. She pulled him inside, her dark eyes shining. "You're just in time for dinner."

It snowed on Thanksgiving morning. The flurries were light, but by noon when Erik and Ana pulled onto the driveway of his parents' house in New Haven, there were two inches on the ground.

In the car, Ana removed her engagement ring and carefully placed it inside a zippered compartment in her handbag. She smiled at Erik who was behind the wheel of the SUV. "Here we go."

They got out and Erik firmly clasped her hand in his as they walked to the house. The door was opened by Isobel who looked smart in navy blue pants and a cream-colored, thick cable-knit sweater. Erik's step-mother hugged him first, then Ana. "We've been wondering when you two would get here."

Erik had noticed Nick and Belana's car in the drive-way, so he and Ana were the last of the out-of-town relatives to arrive. Isobel helped them out of their coats and put them in the foyer closet. "Everyone's in the den," she said. "Come on. Belana and Nick say they have news for us and wouldn't tell us until you got here."

The den was huge with a very high ceiling, crown moldings and furnished with lovely understated contemporary pieces. It was a room designed for the family's comfort and entertainment. A large-screen television was tucked away in a handsome cabinet alongside every other conceivable electronic gadget. Hundreds of DVDs and CDs were shelved next to it. Photos of the family lined the walls and sat atop the grand piano near French doors that led out to one of the gardens.

When Belana spotted Erik and Ana she sprang from her seat on a couch beside her husband, Nick. She hugged Ana. "I haven't seen you in ages, you look so happy!" she said for Ana's ears only.

She was five-four to Ana's five-ten and though Ana towered over her, Belana possessed a quiet strength that belied her size. Initially Belana had taken it upon herself to befriend Ana when Ana had moved to New York because she was her best friend Elle's sister-in-law. However, now, she loved her like a sister of her own.

"So do you," Ana whispered. She let go, so Erik could hug Belana.

The men in the room, John and Nick, stood and kissed Ana on the cheek and shook Erik's hand. Nick's mother, Yvonne and his teen daughter, Nona, were also there.

They also received hugs. Finally, when she could not stand being ignored any longer, Drusilla, who was sitting in a stately Queen Anne chair near the fireplace cleared her throat and tapped her cane on the hardwood floor. "Get over here and give your grandmother some sugar. You, too, Ana Banana!" she demanded.

Ana burst out laughing and hurried over to Drusilla. No one else called her that. She gently kissed Drusilla's soft cheek and let her cheek linger a moment on hers. She loved how Drusilla smelled, like peppermint and pine needles. It was probably something Drusilla rubbed in her joints to combat arthritis, but it reminded Ana of Grandma Renata, and she breathed in deeply. It was funny how smells took you back in time. "How are you, darling?" she asked Drusilla.

Drusilla, only five-one, was wearing one of her tailored suits with a frilly white blouse. She tended toward ultra-feminine attire and even wore gloves winter and summer. She said her hands got cold easily. Ana figured Drusilla didn't feel entirely dressed without them.

Drusilla planted a kiss on her cheek. "I'm fine now that you and Erik are here."

She was wearing her thick glasses today. She had a drawer full, which she chose from depending on how clearly she wanted to see when she got up in the morning. Her son warned her that she should only wear the last pair of glasses her optometrist had prescribed but she had claimed her eyesight changed from day to day. Why shouldn't her glasses? John had finally let it go. There was no winning an argument with his obstinate mother.

She peered closely at Ana's ring finger. There was a faint ring around it. She smiled to herself as Ana moved aside for Erik to hug his grandmother.

Drusilla moaned dramatically when Erik hugged her. She reached up and touched his cheek when he let go of her. Looking into his eyes, she said, "Love becomes you."

Erik was used to his grandmother's enigmatic sayings. This one was somewhat easier to understand than others had been in the past. Clearly she thought being in love suited him. "I couldn't agree more," he said softly.

He and Ana found seats on the couch closest to Drusilla, and Belana stood up, pulling Nick with her. "Happy Thanksgiving, everyone," she began. "I know you're wondering what Nick and I wanted to tell you. First of all, it's good news, not bad. We're not moving or anything. Nobody's sick. Well, I do feel a bit sick sometimes, but the doctor says it'll pass."

With that last sentence Drusilla cried, "Oh, my sweet Lord, are you going to have a baby?"

"Yes!" Belana exclaimed, unable to contain her excitement any longer. She was a dancer and in amazing shape, which was good because she began leaping with joy on those powerful legs and there wasn't much Nick could do to keep her from leaping to the ceiling.

He grabbed her and wrapped her in his arms. "As you can see," he said to everyone in the room. "We're pretty happy about it."

John and Isobel looked at each other and both had tears in their eyes. Elle and Dominic had given them two grandchildren but this would be the first for John's side of the family. They loved being grandparents and now would have a grandchild closer to them since Elle and Dominic lived in Italy.

More hugs and kisses all around.

Things had calmed down quite a bit by the time the housekeeper, Naomi, came into the room and announced that dinner was served.

Everyone rose to go into the dining room. But Drusilla remained seated. She loudly cleared her throat. "Wait I have a question for Erik and Ana before we sit down to eat."

Erik and Ana by eye contact and silent consensus had decided to wait until after dinner to announce their engagement thereby giving Belana and Nick time to savor the love they'd received from the family after their good news.

"What is it?" asked Erik. He stood next to Ana with her hand held in his.

"Was it an engagement ring that left that tan line on Ana's ring finger?" asked Drusilla pointblank.

"What?" asked Belana. She started dancing in place.

Erik and Ana looked at each other, stunned. "How did you spot that?" Erik said.

"I've got my good glasses on," Drusilla informed him. "I don't miss much in these babies."

"That's right, son, she can see through walls in those," said John, amused and curious as to how his son was going to reply to his grandmother's question. "Well, was it an engagement ring?"

Everyone waited impatiently.

Erik pulled Ana in the crook of his arm. "Yes, all right. We're engaged." He smiled at Belana and Nick. "We didn't want to steal your thunder."

"Don't be ridiculous!" his sister said, punching him playfully on the upper arm. "Happy news is always welcome." She grabbed him for a hug, whispering in his ear, "Didn't I tell you the key to her heart was through friendship?"

"Yes, but you didn't mention it would take two years," he returned, grinning.

"Where's the ring," Isobel wanted to know.

Ana removed it from her handbag and put it on. The women crowded around her, admiring it with exclamations of: "It's gorgeous!" and "How lovely."

Drusilla pronounced that it was in good taste. She hated huge ostentatious jewelry. She still was not satisfied, though. She looked suspiciously at Erik and Ana. "There isn't any more good news to share with us, is there?"

"What do you mean?" asked Erik, stumped this time by one of her questions.

She held her right hand out and touched Ana's flat belly. Ana couldn't help laughing.

"No, no, my darling grandmother-to-be," she said. "I'm not pregnant."

"Oh, really, Mother," John complained, his face a mass of smiles. "You are a greedy little woman. Your granddaughter just told you she's making you a great-grandmother and now you want to hurry Erik and Ana along. Be grateful for what you have."

"I'm just saying it would be good news if you were," Drusilla said to Ana. She took Ana's arm and they began walking toward the dining room. "Stranger things have happened," she continued. "I had given up hope of ever having a child when God sent me John…" she trailed off.

Chapter 8

The night of the show arrived before Ana knew it. She had been trying to mentally prepare herself for it but she had sadly failed. Nervousness trumped every other emotion as she and Erik were driven up to the gallery in a hired car.

Damon had warned her that the media would be out in force, and they were. She supposed even in a city as large as New York where celebrities were a dime a dozen, she was news. Three local news stations were represented as well as several online celebrity gossip sites.

She was dressed all in black. A fitted pantsuit that cinched her waist, underneath which was a crisp white shirt open at the collar to reveal a bit of cleavage and platform pumps. With the black overcoat flung across her shoulders she looked smart and stylish. Erik was handsome in a tailored black suit also with a white shirt underneath and dress shoes. He was not wearing a tie tonight, which Ana thought lent him a sexy, roguish air.

Their picture must have been taken dozens of times before they made it safely inside the gallery. Damon greeted them. Ana smiled. "You look wonderful tonight."

"So do you," Damon said, briefly kissing her on both cheeks.

He shook Erik's hand. "Delighted to see you, Erik," he said, his eyes darting around them. He grasped Ana by the hand too tightly. She winced. Something was definitely up with him.

"I have to warn you," he said regrettably, "that Russo is here." He looked behind him before returning his attention to Ana.

She followed his line of sight and saw Jack Russo, surrounded by his entourage, holding court in the back of the room. She noticed that members of his inner circle were effectively keeping the common man from getting too close to him.

She sighed. What the hell was he doing here? Was his career going down the drain so rapidly that he had to put in an appearance at his ex-girlfriend's art exhibit in order to keep the gossips buzzing? Any publicity was good publicity to people like him.

Ana had not voiced any of her thoughts so Damon wasn't sure of what she wanted him to do about Jack

Russo's attendance at the show. "What do you want me to do?" he asked plaintively.

Ana started to suggest he be *tossed out on his ass*. However that kind of behavior would feed the gossip mill more efficiently than a story in which everyone had conducted themselves like mature adults.

She looked to Erik for advice, her eyes somewhat panicked. Erik pulled her close to him reassuringly. "This is your night, sweetheart. Ignore the bastard."

"Then you agree that it would be worse if I made a scene?" Ana wanted his opinion clarified.

"Yes," he confirmed.

Ana hissed to Damon, "But don't sell him any of my work. Nothing, do you understand?"

"Gotcha," said Damon, relief softening his expression. "Let's do this, shall we?"

He stepped up to the podium that had been set up in the middle of the huge showroom. A path of what appeared to be yellow brick but what was in fact made of a hard slip-resistant plastic, made a path through the gallery. Ana smiled when she saw it: Damon's yellow-brick road from *The Wizard of Oz*.

"Ladies and gentlemen, may I present the very talented artist, Ms. Ana Corelli!"

The room was packed. Ana saw many faces she knew like the Barones from Bridgeport, Connecticut, and many friends she'd made in her career as a model. Jack Russo wasn't the only actor there. There were several New York City actors whom she knew from Broadway. More interesting to her were the people she did not know or who had no reason to be there except being lovers of art.

Damon had assured her that she would not have to answer questions, simply wave to the crowd and fade into the background while her work was being perused. After she had joined him at the podium and smiled at everyone and mouthed, *Thank you for coming,* she and Erik then joined the Barones.

Teresa and Julianna hugged Ana, and Erik and Leo shook hands. "I knew you were talented but this is outrageous," Teresa said to Ana, gesturing to the general bedlam in the showroom. "We almost didn't get in."

"I have to have the painting of the elderly man in the tattered coat," Leo said. "Who is he? His face has such character."

"He's a homeless gentleman I met a few years ago," Ana told him. "Proceeds from the paintings are going to help fund several New York City organizations that help the homeless."

"Good cause," said Leo.

"Leo, if you want that painting, you need to go make an offer to that lovely man who introduced himself to us when we arrived," Teresa told him. "Otherwise someone is going to beat you to it."

Leo looked concerned. "Yes, I'd better do that." He regarded Ana and Erik. "Excuse us."

The Barones went in search of Damon.

Ana and Erik weren't alone for long. From behind them came a well-modulated voice. "Ana, darling, aren't you going to say hello after I went to all the trouble of attending your first art show?"

Ana schooled her expression before turning to face Jack Russo. He was as she remembered him. Tall, dark and handsome, a Hollywood cliché expensively attired in a dark designer suit. His Italian ancestors had come from southern Italy so he was swarthy with dark, soulful eyes. His black hair was curly and he wore it overly long because he thought it looked sexy. Personally, she had always thought he should cut it and look more groomed.

With a flick of his wrist, he signaled his hangers-on to disperse, denoting he wanted to speak privately with Ana. The look he gave Ana after told her he expected her to do likewise with Erik.

Instead she smiled and said, "Jack Russo meet Erik Whitaker, my fiancé."

All his years of pretending to be someone else had not prepared Jack Russo for this. Erik and Ana had not made any public announcements of their engagement, only among family and friends, so Ana wasn't surprised he was shocked. Perhaps he expected her to still be alone, pining for him.

He laughed nervously. "I had no idea."

"You wouldn't expect me to send you a text message, would you?"

He did not miss her dig. "No, I wouldn't," he said. He regarded Erik and offered his hand. "Congratulations."

Erik firmly shook his hand and promptly let go of it. "Thank you."

Ana was done with niceties, although she vowed not to raise her voice. "What are you doing here?"

Jack gestured to one of her paintings. "I never knew you painted. When I read about the show I had to come see for myself. Little Ana whom we all thought was just a pretty face is also a talented artist. Good for you. I'm proud of you."

Ana was delighted to learn that his opinion meant nothing to her. In fact, peering closely at him, she wondered what she ever saw in him. Could it be she had been as shallow as he was? She had chosen to subject herself to him based solely on looks?

That had to be it. She could only conclude that she had grown over the years and he had remained the same. Because now all she saw was someone who had so little substance he had to rely on the elusive thing called fame in order to feel good about himself.

Here in this showroom, he was the center of attention. She saw the other patrons gawking at him, probably wondering what he was saying to her right now, his ex-girlfriend as some of them were undoubtedly well aware.

Suddenly, all of the hurt and anger that she had felt upon seeing him here dissipated. She no longer felt irritated by his presence.

She actually smiled at him and said, "Thank you, Jack, that's very sweet of you. Now, if you'll excuse us, we really should circulate."

She and Erik left him standing there. Of course he wasn't alone for long. His entourage again formed a

protective circle around him and when he began talking, hung on his every word.

Erik pulled her close and kissed her cheek. "You're
a class act."

Ana was about to say something to Erik when she
noticed his parents coming through the door followed
by Belana and Nick. "Our family's here," she said, and
they made a beeline over to them.

Ana enjoyed herself from that moment on. Damon
sold all of her paintings except the one of Drusilla in
the garden, which was not for sale at any price.

He also told her that before Jack Russo had left the
gallery he had offered a substantial amount for her self-
portrait. Damon had claimed someone else had already
purchased it. From the miffed expression on the handsome actor's face, Damon related, he had not believed
him for a moment. That was when he had stormed out,
followed by his lackeys.

Later, Erik took her home. Their footsteps made
clicking sounds on the hardwood floor as they made
their way back to the bedroom. Clothes were removed
in the dark with only the streetlights lending little illu-
mination through the slats in the blinds.

Erik pulled her warm body into his strong arms.
Their kisses were tender, lingering and so intoxicat-
ing. She fell back onto the bed, pulling him on top of
her. Her legs wrapped themselves around him as she
guided him inside of her. Urgently the passion rose as
his thrusts deepened, touching her very core. A sob
tore from her throat as she reached the crescendo, and

Erik followed seconds later. They lay like that for a few minutes, his nose buried in the side of her neck. They trembled in ecstasy and soon found a more comfortable position but were not willing to let go too soon.

The next day Damon phoned her with good news. "I've gotten five requests from people who want you to paint them."

Ana was standing in the kitchen, stirring soft-scrambled eggs in a skillet. She reached over and turned off the flame under the skillet before replying, "You mean commissions?" She had heard of them but never considered that someone would want to hire her to paint them even though she knew that sort of thing came with the territory once word got around that you were talented.

"Who wants me to paint them?" she asked excitedly as she one-handedly slid the scrambled eggs onto a plate. Erik was in the shower. She had gotten up about an hour earlier and was already showered and dressed. It was a Sunday morning and they didn't have any commitments. They were planning on taking a leisurely walk around the city if it didn't snow today, perhaps do a little window shopping. December in New York was beautiful. And the closer to Christmas the more festive the displays in store windows became.

Damon named three people in the performing arts community in the city: two actors and a well-known soprano with the Metropolitan Opera, and the addition of two politicians.

"I don't know," Ana said. "I've never even thought of

doing something like that. *I* always choose my subjects. I don't even know if painting someone at their request would inspire me. It's not like a quick sketch that you can do in a matter of minutes. Painting a portrait takes days of effort and if I'm not feeling it I don't know if I can produce a decent portrait."

"Artists," Damon said. "The problem with artists today is none are starving anymore. When artists were starving they took commissions hand over fist because wanting to know where your next meal was coming from was inspiring. Think about it, darling. The more you earn, the more you can donate to the needy. Besides, I look at taking commissions as a way to build your reputation in the art community. If you later find you don't like doing it, you can always stop."

"I'll think about it," Ana agreed. "I've got to go. Thank you, Damon, for everything. Last night wasn't as frightening as I thought it would be."

Damon laughed. "I told you all you had to do was show up and be yourself. Your work would speak for itself."

Erik strode into the kitchen barefooted wearing jeans and a long-sleeve shirt. He came straight to Ana and began kissing her. She held the phone away from them but she was certain Damon could probably hear what was going on. Erik sounded like a starving man, moaning like crazy, eliciting the same response from her with his intensity. She managed to break off the kiss long enough to say into the receiver, "Gotta go!" She heard Damon laughing uproariously before she put the phone down on the counter and resumed kissing Erik.

"Good morning," said Erik, after he'd rendered her nearly breathless. His smile was electric. Ana loved seeing him like this: ready to take on the day, his attitude confident and infectious.

"Good morning," she said, her smile as wide as his. "How did you sleep?"

"Like the dead but, I swear, I could sense when you got out of bed."

Erik hadn't let go of her yet. And he obviously was not finished kissing her as his warm lips continued to leave a trail of kisses along the side of her neck. Ana was beginning to get the message. But the little Catholic girl in her was leery of where this might be headed, making love in the kitchen. She was enjoying their love life but there were still certain taboos she had no desire to break and making love on the kitchen counter or the kitchen table was one of them. Growing up she would have been traumatized if she had walked into the kitchen and found her parents making love on the table where they all sat down and had their meals.

She laughed nervously and turned out of his embrace. "Come on, let's eat. I made scrambled eggs and there's bread for toast, orange juice and, of course, coffee. I need to go shopping, the cupboard's nearly bare." Sometimes she talked too much when she was uneasy.

Picking up on her mood, Erik asked, "Is something the matter?"

She decided to tell him the truth. "I don't want to get overheated in the kitchen."

He laughed and reached down to smooth her brow the way he did when he's about to kiss her. Ana waited, then just as he was lowering his head to kiss her she twisted out of his embrace and Erik, off balance, stumbled and righted himself by pushing against the granite counter. By the time he turned around to face her, Ana was standing three feet away with her arms folded, giving him a stern look. "Don't play with me, Erik Whitaker. I told you—not in the kitchen."

With a determined expression, Erik went and picked her up and began walking in the direction of the bedroom. "All right, then, the bedroom it is."

"I'm hungry!" Ana protested, laughter evident in her tone.

"I'll take you out for breakfast afterward," Erik promised.

"We just got out of bed," she cried. "Aren't you ever satisfied?"

"Not when it comes to you," he said, pushing the bedroom door open.

They were both laughing by the time he put her down. "Look at you," she said as she unbuttoned his shirt, "showered and dressed and now you're going to get all funky again."

"Yes," he breathed lustily, apparently looking forward to being dirtied up by her and vice versa. That mischievous glint in his eye told her she was right.

"Oh, I know what this is," she said as he pulled her

sweater over her head and turned her around so that he could unfasten her bra. "I'm a fast learner. I might not know much about men and sex, but I do know you get horny in the mornings. I've noticed…things…but was too shy to talk about them with you."

Erik took her hand and put it on his hard member. "You mean this thing? You've noticed this thing in the mornings?"

Ana blushed but didn't try to remove her hand. "You're a corrupting influence," she lightly accused him. "If I stay with you much longer I'm going to know everything there is to know about pleasing a man."

"Well, this man, anyway," Erik said and bent to take one of her nipples, which he'd recently liberated from her bra into his mouth. Ana moaned and her bones seemed to turn to jelly. She fell backward onto the bed, which she hadn't yet had the chance to make this morning, and her fiancé made short work of removing her jeans and panties. This done, he gently spread her legs and touched her sex with the palm of his hand and moved it in small circles, enjoying the warmth and the feel of it. Her clitoris became aroused and as soon as he felt the wetness on his palm he used his index finger to further stimulate it while Ana writhed beneath him.

"Don't be afraid to express your sexual desires to me, Ana," he softly said as he continued his efforts. "You're safe with me. Let go of your inhibitions."

Ana sighed with pleasure as she tried to construct sentences in her head, sentences that he would understand. She liked sex as well as any other woman but the full enjoyment of sex, the letting go of her inhibitions seemed contrary to her Catholic upbringing. She remembered going to mass with her Grandma Renata and always being admonished to stay pure until marriage. That ship had definitely sailed. In these modern times women didn't save themselves for marriage as often as they used to. At least that's the general consensus she'd gotten from talking to other women of her generation. But if you were smart, you didn't sleep around, either. You tried to choose wisely. She hadn't chosen wisely until now.

She relaxed. Erik was right, she was safe with him. She could be herself and stop holding back, because that's what she had been doing. She looked him in the eyes, and said, "Aren't you forgetting something? I'm naked, splayed on the bed for your pleasure but you still have your pants on."

Erik rose and rectified the situation with rapidity. He stood before her without any clothes on. She got up and kissed him all the while backing him toward the bed. When he was in position, she placed her palm in the middle of his muscular chest and pushed him onto the bed. Climbing on top, she cooed, "Let me drive awhile."

Erik chuckled, remembering how much she liked to drive. It could prove interesting to see what she considered driving in the bedroom, little innocent girl that she was.

As he lay flat on his back Ana bent and licked him down the middle of his chest from his breastbone to his naval. His eyes never left her. Perhaps that was his fatal mistake. He would try later to recall every move Ana made.

"Mmm, you taste good," she said, her eyes looking directly into his. She held his attention like a cobra holds a snake charmer's. Then she straddled him and began rubbing her breasts until her nipples hardened. This by itself was an erotic feast for Erik since he was a breast man and hers were magnificent. But when she bent and flicked her tongue out and licked her own nipples, first the right then the left, his member jumped of its own accord.

That was only the beginning. After she had enticed him with a demonstration of her flexibility, she scooted backward and since he was fully engorged now his penis stood straight up and she took what was offered. Her mouth below was almost his undoing. She made him beg her to stop because he was afraid if she didn't he'd come and he didn't want this lovemaking session to end without Ana being satisfied. He always made sure of that.

She smiled coyly at him as she got up to get a condom. Returning to him she rolled it onto him and straddled him. She was so wet by this time that when her sex touched the tip of his penis all he wanted to do was slide inside and experience the ultimate in pleasure. But she worked her vaginal muscles so that she was the one controlling how far he could enter her. She allowed him entrance inch by inch, squeezing him and causing ripples of anticipatory sexual enjoyment to fan out from his member to the rest of his body. God help him, the girl was curling his toes. Where the hell had she learned that? Then, just as he had gained a little control and felt confident that he wouldn't embarrass himself by coming too soon, she pushed hard and impaled herself on him.

She cried out because he could tell he'd hit her sweet spot. He yelled because she'd caught him off guard and there was no turning back now. He came and he felt as if the tip of the condom wouldn't be able to hold it all. That's how good the release had felt.

She lay on top of him, her head on his chest. He felt her pulsating vaginal walls as she came down from the climax. She felt him throb inside of her. Their eyes met. "Where did you learn that?" he asked curiously.

"The *Kama Sutra*," she told him smiling. "I like to read, remember?"

Chapter 9

A few days before Christmas Ana phoned her parents to catch up. She had already told them she was staying in the States for Christmas, and they had expressed disappointment but said they understood she wanted to spend time with Erik. They were not the kind of parents who put added pressure on their children in the form of guilt. For that she was grateful.

"Is Dad preparing dinner this year, or will you go to one of my aunts' houses?" she asked her mother.

"Dominic and Elle invited us to Lake Como, so we'll be going there," Natalie told her. "Elle's going to prepare a traditional soul food meal for us. I'm supposed to get in the kitchen with her. We'll see how that works out. And I don't think your father can do without his panettone at Christmastime. He'll be baking at least a couple of loaves."

"Can't say that I blame him," Ana said with a smile. The traditional sweet loaf that originated in Milan was a family staple. Cupola-shaped and made with raisins, candied orange, citron and lemon zest, it was wrapped with care and put under the Christmas tree and enjoyed later in the evening with coffee or sweet wine.

"You sound kind of wistful," Natalie told her. "Is everything all right between you and Erik?"

Ana sighed happily. "Mom, I'm so in love with that man it feels unreal. I'm afraid I'm going to wake up one morning and find out it was all a dream."

Natalie laughed softly. "Baby, you're in the giddy stage of your relationship. Of course it feels dreamlike. You're so happy you think you might explode. He can do no wrong, you can do no wrong. And the sex…well the sex blows your mind. I've been there."

Ana was not embarrassed to discuss sex with her mother. It was her father with whom she never broached the subject.

"You're right," she confirmed. "I've never felt this way before."

"How could you?" asked Natalie reasonably. "You've never been in love before. Not really." She paused. "Yes, it's Ana, sweetheart."

Her father, Carlo, must have entered the room.

He came on the line. *"Buon Natale!"* he exclaimed in his deep, Italian-accented voice. "In case I don't get to speak with you on Christmas."

"Daddy, I don't care where I am in the world, I will find a way to speak with you on Christmas Day," Ana assured him. A tear rolled down her cheek, her father was so dear to her. She was the baby of the family and he had always made sure that she knew she was special and could depend on her old man, as he referred to himself, for anything.

She imagined his sweet face now: tanned skin, a full head of wavy dark brown hair with pieces of gray throughout, that Roman nose and a chin with a cleft in it. No wonder her mother had fallen in love with him on first sight.

She sniffed. "I'm coming home next Christmas, promise!"

Carlo laughed shortly. "Now, none of that or *Babbo Natale* will not visit you this Christmas. Stay cheerful, darling. We'll see you soon."

She smiled. She'd loved his *Babbo Natale*—Father Christmas—stories when she was a little girl. Point in fact: she *still* loved them.

"Okay," she said. He invariably ended their conversations with "We'll see you soon." As if she had only a short length of time to wait before she saw them again even though she knew that it would probably be months.

"Yes, see you soon, Dad," Ana said.

After she'd hung up the phone she got up from the couch where she'd been sitting in the living room and walked to the big picture window, which looked down on the busy street in front of her building. Pedestrians hurried to their destinations carrying shopping bags. It was dusk and lights were going on in windows of neighboring apartments. Christmas decorations predominated. She had framed her windows with tiny twinkling white lights and in the center of it was the huge fir tree strung with colorful lights.

She and Erik had decorated trees at her place and his. She was glad he enjoyed the custom as much as she did. She couldn't imagine Christmas without a tree.

Shrugging her shoulders as if she could shake off this melancholy feeling, she turned away from the window and walked to the kitchen where she got herself a bottle of water and thirstily drank half of it standing in front of the refrigerator. She had no reason to feel sad, yet the feeling persisted. Surely it wasn't because she wasn't going home for Christmas. She was an adult now and adults grew up, moved away from home, met someone and got married. From then on your first priority was your mate. Yes, you spent time with your extended family, but if you couldn't make it home for the holidays you didn't beat yourself up about it.

This is the first time, she reminded herself that was why she wasn't handling it so well.

Tomorrow she and Erik were flying to Aspen. They would spend December 23 through December 26 there. Then they would toast in the New Year here in New York with his family who would be coming to his penthouse for the annual Whitaker New Year's Eve party, an end of the year blowout where the family and employees of Whitaker Enterprises mingled. She had looked forward to the party every year. This year would be different because she wouldn't be coming as a guest, but as Erik's fiancée. She was even planning it this year, she had hired the caterer and the entertainment for the evening. They were going to dance the night away to the sounds of the best blues band in New York City. Then just before midnight they were going to tune in to the yearly broadcast of the ball dropping in Times Square on the big-screen TV.

Setting the bottle of water on the counter she went to her studio and pulled the drop cloth off her work in progress. It was a portrait of Erik in the nude. He was sitting in the classic pose of *The Thinker* by Auguste Rodin. There was nothing explicit about it. But the lines and planes of his body were very seductive. He didn't know she was painting it. She'd done it from memory. She knew his body intimately and loved it not only because she loved him but because of its symmetry. She didn't know how he would react to it. She had no intention of ever selling it or even allowing it to be shown at Damon's gallery. This was a gift for her. It would hang in her bedroom when it was complete.

She heard Erik's key in the lock. They had exchanged keys more than a year ago for safety purposes. If either of them were in trouble and couldn't answer their door the other would have a means of entry. They even knew each other's security codes. She smiled at the thought. That should have tipped her off that she and Erik were meant to be more than just friends. How implicitly they trusted each other.

"Babe, I'm home!"

She hastily covered the painting with the drop cloth before hurrying to him. Erik was already coming out of his overcoat when she got to the foyer. She helped him off with it and hung it up then went into his arms for a long kiss. It was during the kiss that her hands wandered to his head and she discovered his hair was damp. "Is it raining?"

"No, it's snowing," he said, grinning.

"What!" Ana ran to the window to look out. Sure enough snowflakes drifted down covering the city with a white mantle. She was delighted. Erik came up behind her and wrapped his arms around her. "We're gonna have a white Christmas, after all."

The weather service had been doubtful the last few days whenever they tuned in to the forecast.

"Looks like it," Ana said, smiling happily.

"You call this a cabin?" Ana asked Erik as the hired car pulled into the driveway leading up to what Ana thought looked more like a Swiss chalet than a cabin. It was dark out but she could see that the multilevel house was at least three stories and must have been five thousand square feet or more. Were those Christmas lights she saw in the windows? Snow was coming down pretty heavily but she didn't think her eyes were deceiving her. "Who decorated it?" she asked Erik, who was being suspiciously quiet all of a sudden. He'd chatted all the way from the airport.

The driver stopped the SUV fitted with snow tires in front of the chalet's awning. "Did you hire someone to prepare the house before we arrived?" Ana asked, looking at Erik. These vacation rentals sometimes had people who stocked the refrigerator for renters, cleaned and aired out the house and changed the bed linens. Why not decorate it for the holidays, too? "What's wrong, cat got your tongue?" Ana asked irritably. Something was up. She hated surprises and was learning, fast, that her fiancé loved surprising her. The way he'd sprung the ring on her had been hard enough on her heart. What girl picked out a ring from Tiffany's in her man's office?

She reached for the door's handle. The driver had already gotten out and was getting their luggage. Erik grabbed her hand before she could open the door. "Sweetheart, no matter what happens the next few minutes remember I love you." He looked at her gravely.

Frowning, Ana regarded him with a worried expression. "Now you're making me nervous. What have you done?"

"Let me get the door for you," was all he said before he got out and jogged around to her side of the SUV to open the door and help her out. He made sure she didn't slip on the snow as she stood on shaky legs. She hugged herself in her warm coat. The car had been warm but it was freezing out here. The driver was busy piling their luggage on the portico. Solar lights lit the path to the door. Erik rang the doorbell.

"Why are you ringing the doorbell?" asked Ana. "Don't you have the key?" Erik had handled the reservations for this trip. She assumed if he were renting a cabin the key would be sent to him prior to their departure from New York or someone representing the owner would meet them either at the airport or here with the key. Which hadn't happened, so where was the key?

"I don't need a key," he said cryptically.

Ana heard someone coming to the door. In fact it sounded like the rumble of several excited voices approaching.

The door was swung open and her mother and father stood there smiling at her. Elle, Dominic and Sophia and Matteo, each of them with a child, not far behind them. Ana screamed and launched herself at her parents whom she hugged together, with her in the middle and a parent on either side of her. She let them go and regarded them. Everyone was dressed casually. Her father had an apron on over his clothes. It's obvious who's been delegated to do the cooking, as usual, Ana thought with a smile. "I just spoke with you a few hours ago. You couldn't have come from Milan in that short time!"

Her mother helped her out of her coat and hung it on a nearby hall tree.

"No, baby, you phoned my cell number. We were here all along," Natalie said, smiling warmly. Natalie's rich brown skin glowed with good health and her dark brown eyes shone with happiness.

Ana hugged her brother, Dominic, her sister, Sophia, and their spouses as her mother continued, "Erik wanted to surprise you so we flew in yesterday. The house was all ready for us. Everything provided. We've just been enjoying ourselves getting ready for your arrival."

Ana kissed each niece and nephew, longing to hold the babies, but reluctant to take them out of the comfortable embrace of their parents' arms. Elle must have read her indecision on her face and thrust her four-month-old son, Dom, into his aunt's arms.

"Here, take him," she said. "Hold him close to your chest. He loves bosoms." She glanced at her husband, Dominic, when she said that and Ana laughed as she cradled her nephew in her arms. He grinned up at her looking for all the world like a miniature replica of her brother, dimples in his cheeks and curious glint in his light brown eyes as if he knew that life was a mystery he was going to have a ball solving.

She bent and kissed his chubby cheeks, "Hello, little Dominic, I'm your auntie Ana."

Her two nieces, Ariana and Renata, were both two but Ariana was a few months older than her cousin, Renata, suddenly felt the need to exert their claim on their aunt Ana since they had known her longer. They each latched on to one of Ana's legs and refused to budge. Then, sensing he was being left out of the fun, six month-old Matteo, in his father's arms, started crying and reaching for Ana.

Ana laughed happily. "It's good to be loved!" And holding little Dom to her chest she bent close and kissed Matty who stopped crying and stared at her, then looked at his mother.

"Oh, no, he's confused," laughed Sophia. She and Ana could never be mistaken for twins but, being sisters, they did closely resemble each other. They had the same golden brown skin, golden brown eyes and full lips. But Ana was taller and wore her hair in a wavy style while her sister preferred a braid, which hung nearly to her bottom.

Erik came into the house while all of this was going on after taking care of the driver's tip and bringing in the luggage. A smile of satisfaction tugged at the corners of his mouth. Ana was happy. He owed Abby a debt of thanks, which would be reflected in her bonus this year. He'd asked her to work a miracle, and she had.

Seeing that Erik had entered the house, Ana gingerly handed the baby back to Elle. As he closed the door, Ana came up behind him and as soon as he turned around she walked into his arms and kissed him with all the emotion she was feeling at that moment. That kiss left no doubt in his mind that she was grateful for his gesture.

Carlo loudly cleared his throat. Seeing his baby girl kiss a man like that was too much for a father to bear. Even though he knew, logically, that he would eventually have to let go of her, it wasn't that time yet. "Come, Ana, you and your old man are making the panettone together this year. Plus, there's dinner to get on the table."

Ana was so accustomed to helping her father prepare meals at home that the thought of slipping into the routine now was a very pleasant one.

Ana smiled up at Erik before turning to join her father, *"Ti amo,"* she said.

"I love you, too," Erik said, his love for her emanating from every cell of his body.

He was welcomed into the Corelli family's embrace while he watched his fiancée put her arm through her father's and accompany him to the kitchen.

When Ana and Carlo were out of earshot, Natalie helped Erik out of his coat and hung it next to Ana's then she gave Erik a hug and said, "Forgive Carlo, but in this family he wears the apron and he's not ready to cut the strings yet where Ana is concerned." She peered up at him. "But that doesn't mean he doesn't like you. He does. He just doesn't like it when you get too close to his daughter in his presence. It's primal. You'll understand when you're a father of a daughter."

Erik chuckled. "Thanks for the tip. I'll behave myself accordingly."

"See? I knew you were a smart man," said Sophia. She hugged him, too. Then she stepped aside for Elle to embrace him. Erik had considered Elle a sister ever since their parents were married. "Hello, sis," he murmured against her ear. "Motherhood definitely agrees with you." Elle had given birth to Dominic, Jr. a little over four months ago. Tonight she looked wonderful in a red long-sleeved wrap blouse over black slacks. She'd lost all the baby weight except for a little around her middle. She smiled up at him, "I have to agree with that." She glanced back at her husband. "If he had his way we'd have a house full."

Dominic shook Erik's hand. He couldn't help remembering that the first time he met Erik, he had pulled him aside to say that he had had a crush on Elle for years but she wouldn't give him the time of day because she was such good friends with Erik's sister, Belana, and hence considered him a brother. How time manipulated events. Now Erik was going to be his brother-in-law!

"Good to see you again," Dominic said. "I hope this will give us a chance to get to know each other better."

Sophia interrupted to introduce her husband, Matteo, whom Erik had not met before.

After shaking hands with Matteo and hearing his thick Italian accent Erik realized that there was quite a multicultural mix in this house tonight. He was African-American, as were Natalie and Elle. Carlo and Matteo were Italian and the offspring of Carlo and Natalie: Dominic, Sophia and Ana were half Italian and half African-American. To say nothing of the four children whom he hadn't been introduced to yet who also had a mixture of African and Italian blood.

Ariana and Renata regarded Erik with the assessment of little girls who although they don't yet understand it felt drawn to male beauty. They each took one of his hands and Erik smiled down at them respectively and said, "Hello, ladies."

"Meet Renata and Ariana," Natalie said, laughing softly at how easily her granddaughters had accepted Erik. "Come back to the entertainment room. We were in there watching a movie with the children when you rang the bell. While Carlo prepares dinner."

In the kitchen, Ana had washed her hands and put on an apron. Her father talked while he checked the pots on the stove and peeked at the roast in the oven. "So, how are you enjoying being an engaged woman?"

Ana was instantly on alert. Her father might have been asking an innocent enough question. On the other hand it could be a loaded one. How she answered would make all the difference in the world. "We were friends for a long time before we considered anything romantic. He knew he had to be patient with me."

"You're a little shy," said Carlo dismissively. "You've always been that way."

He had moved over to the center island, which had been cleared of everything except the ingredients he needed to make the panettone. Ana joined him and watched as he began sifting flour into a large bowl. "No, it was more than that, Daddy. I didn't trust my own judgment anymore. Erik knew that and didn't try to push me into a relationship even though, he told me later, he's been in love with me all along."

Her father set down the sifter and looked her in the eyes. He had known she had gotten her heart broken by that actor. He couldn't remember his name. As a rule he avoided gossip about his daughter like the plague. Gossip was insidious. Tabloids made up lies about celebrities. Terrible lies that any relative of the subject of such tales didn't want to hear.

"Has he behaved like a gentleman the whole time?" he asked.

"Yes, he did," Ana replied sincerely. "He's been my best friend for two years."

"And when did you know you loved him, as well?" her father wanted to know.

Ana hadn't even told Erik about the moment she realized she loved him. She began to recall the instant in which her emotions transformed from "like" to love for Erik. They were jogging in Central Park one Saturday morning in May of last year. She tripped and fell. She still didn't know what she had tripped over, just her own stupid feet she guessed. But she twisted her ankle and Erik had picked her up and carried her to a nearby cab and had taken her directly to the emergency room of the closest hospital. He had refused to leave her side for three hours while they waited. It seemed a twisted ankle did not warrant quick treatment. He had told her funny stories about his visits to the emergency room when he was a kid. He had not always been such a good athlete. When he was a boy he was clumsy, awkward, and constantly hurting himself. Once playing baseball he got hit in the face by a fly ball. Another time he and a neighborhood friend decided they were going to become Noble Prize–winning chemists. They mixed the wrong chemicals and nearly choked to death on billowing black smoke. They were lucky the mixture hadn't exploded in their faces. The smoke had stained the walls of his bedroom, though, and the entire room had to be repainted. His father banned him from using his chemistry set in the house after that. Lucky, too, because the next time he'd used it, he had indeed caused an explosion that resulted in the detached garage being burned to the ground.

"Your father had to have taken away your chemistry set then," she'd exclaimed in disbelief.

"No, but he did make me clean the debris out of the

garage so it could be rebuilt. It took me three weeks. I was the one who decided to give up the chemistry set and turn my attentions to something safer, like computers."

"He has a doctorate degree in computer science," Ana told her father now. Her expression grew wistful. "I couldn't help loving a man who had been such a geek growing up and had turned himself into such an accomplished person."

"You respect him," said Carlo.

"Yes," Ana said softly.

Carlo picked up the sifter again. "This is good," he said, "the fact that you respect him as well as love him. That will be good for your marriage because the intensity of romance you feel right now won't last. Sometimes you will feel such passion you will think that you'll die if you spend an hour apart. Then again sometimes you will wish you'd never met him." He chuckled. "I can see by your doubtful expression that you don't believe me. Take my word for it. Marriage is a lifelong commitment and it isn't something to be trifled with. When you say 'I do' to Erik you have to mean it. So many marriages end in divorce because the couple was not truly committed to each other before they tied the knot. Then they start living together and closeness breeds contempt. You will begin to find out personal things about him that you didn't know before you married him."

"What kind of things?" asked Ana, her tone light, matching her father's.

She figured he was trying to scare her into thinking twice before marrying Erik. She knew her father would be a hard sell no matter whom she decided to marry. No one, in his opinion, was good enough for her. He had felt the same way about Sophia's choice in a husband even though Sophia and Matteo had dated for over five years before Matteo proposed. Poor Sophia had assumed that Matteo was reluctant to propose because she was such a strong-willed woman, plus she earned more money than he did and probably always would. Matteo owned a landscaping business. He worked wonders in gardens. He was a sweet, caring man who fell in love with Sophia, and then found out she stood to inherit millions, a prospect that was quite daunting to a simple man like him. Sophia, however, would not let him go. She was of the mind that it was better to be loved by a man of modest means than to be used by a rich man. She didn't need her bank account bolstered. What she needed was a man who adored her, and she got him.

Carlo looked intently at his daughter. "That he farts in bed and talks with food in his mouth," he said jokingly, "Things that irritate feminine sensibilities. Men can be quite barbaric at times. At those times you have to remember that you love him and overlook the small things."

Ana laughed abruptly. "I was wrong. You're not trying to convince me to think twice before getting married, you're giving me advice."

Carlo put a hand over his heart. "You thought that

your old man would do such a despicable thing? I feel hurt!"

"I didn't expect you to be so accepting of Erik," Ana said truthfully. She could tell by the pent-up laughter in her father's eyes that he wasn't really upset by anything she'd said. "You made Sophia cry when you told her she shouldn't marry Matteo."

"I only said that because Matteo wasn't sure of himself," Carlo explained. "In order for a man to commit to a woman, he must first know his own heart. Matteo was afraid he wouldn't fit in Sophia's world. He doubted himself. Now he knows we love him for who he is, not for what he can bring to the table. Their marriage is solid. I didn't get that feeling from Erik. He knows what he wants. He was patient enough to wait for you. That says a lot about a man."

"Oh, Daddy, I'm so happy you feel that way!" Ana flung her arms around his waist and hugged him.

Carlo got misty-eyed. "Hey, we're wasting time here. Let's get this panettone ready for the oven. You know it has to be made a day in advance before it's ready to place under the tree. It's going to take longer than you think."

That was an understatement as Ana was to learn. The panettone took a total of fifteen hours to make from mixing bowl to oven. While they waited for the panettone to rise, the family caught up with each other's lives.

Chapter 10

Dinner was a savory meal of minestrone soup, roast beef, and crusty Italian bread. Afterward the couples with children gathered their little ones to prepare them for bed.

Carlo and Natalie with Ana and Erik made short work of clearing the table and cleaning the kitchen. While they worked, Natalie told Ana and Erik about the chores chart they had made upon arriving at the house yesterday. Erik had offered to hire someone to come in and cook and clean for them the three days they would be together, but the Corellis had graciously declined saying they were capable of taking care of themselves and that it would be fun to divide up the meals.

As Natalie dried dishes, she filled Ana in. "You and Erik have breakfast tomorrow morning at nine."

"No problem," said Ana, smiling at Erik. "Erik makes delicious pancakes and I'm a whiz at scrambled eggs and bacon."

"Sounds great," said Natalie.

With the dishes done, they all retired to the entertainment room. As soon as they sat down, Carlo asked, "Have you thought about where you want to get married?"

Ana, sitting close to Erik on a couch near the fireplace, smiled at him. "We've talked about it. But Erik says he doesn't care where we get married. He thinks I should have the wedding of my dreams and to just give him the time and date and he'll show up."

Carlo chuckled. "It would save time and money," he agreed. Ana hoped her mother had missed that surreptitious look her father had given her.

Natalie had not, and playfully elbowed her husband in the ribs. "Quit it. I was not that bossy about our wedding plans."

"Darling, you wanted things a certain way and when you didn't get your way you pouted," Carlo recalled. His eyebrows were raised as if to say, "Deny it."

Natalie laughed. "Okay, I was a bit…forceful about getting my way. But in my defense I did have your mother and your sisters to contend with and every last one of them had a vision of what our wedding should be like. I didn't think that was fair since it was our wedding!"

"I hear you, sweetheart," consoled Carlo. "Didn't I

not make it clear to them that it was our wedding not theirs?"

Natalie leaned her head on his shoulder. "You did, indeed."

"But I don't agree with Erik," Ana said, getting the conversation back on track. "I think the wedding should be his dream wedding, too."

"I've already got my dream girl. I'm satisfied," said Erik.

"Aren't they sweet?" Natalie cried wistfully.

"Aren't who sweet?" Sophia asked as she entered the room with Matteo.

"We were talking about our wedding plans," Ana told her.

Sophia and Matteo sat on the couch facing Ana and Erik. "You're coming home to get married, aren't you?" said Sophia expectantly. "Mom and Dad got married in the garden at the Lake Como villa, so did Dominic and Elle and Matteo and I. You're not going to stick to family tradition?"

"Lake Como *is* my first choice," Ana admitted. "But we haven't decided yet whether it would be more cost effective for my family to fly to the States or for my friends who live in the States plus Erik's family and friends to come all the way to Italy. Erik's parents have a very nice garden in Connecticut."

Erik could see how wedding negotiations could dissolve into an argument. Sophia's expression was none too friendly. She was looking at him now like he was the wedge that was keeping her family apart.

"You're not wearing a Corelli original, either?" Sophia asked as if Ana's not wearing a dress from her family's formal wear line would be the ultimate betrayal of familial loyalty.

"Yes, I'm wearing a Corelli original," Ana said. She had already been offered free wedding dresses by some of the best designers in the world. People whom she respected and who respected her. But she had declined. "I've already picked out my dress."

"Which one?" her father wanted to know. In his mind he kept a catalog of all his new merchandise. "Let me guess. The simple silk strapless empire-waist gown with pearl buttons down the back?"

"How did you know that?" asked Ana, amazed.

"I pictured you in that very dress," said Carlo, smiling.

Her father had an uncanny knack for choosing clothing that looked good on people.

"Well, I'll be campaigning for you to get married in Lake Como," Sophia said stubbornly.

"I'm sorry, sis, but you don't get a say in this," Ana said just as stubbornly. "Did I dictate to you how your wedding should be?"

"No," Sophia said, her voice now taking on a whiny tone, "but you're away from home all the time. I miss you! It would be nice if you, me, Mom, and the females in the family could get together and plan your wedding, that's all."

Elle and Dominic entered the room at that instance and Elle smiled and said, "Are we planning the wedding? When is it going to be? Where? Do I have time to finish losing weight so I can get in a decent dress?"

"Elle you look beautiful just the way you are," Ana told her sincerely. "And, yes, we're talking about the wedding, but no plans have been made."

Elle and Dominic sat down on the sofa with Carlo and Natalie. "Just tell us where it will be and we'll be there," said Dominic. "And take it from me, baby sister, keep it simple. Planning a wedding can tear a couple apart. Everybody wants to give you advice. It starts with the best of intentions, of course, but can turn ugly at the drop of a hat. I say, don't listen to anyone except Erik when it comes to how you two want to get married. Do it in a church. Do it on a boat. Do it at the courthouse, or on the beach. But do it your way."

"Yes," Elle said in agreement. "I was lucky. Our wedding was simple and elegant and everybody we loved was there."

"That's all that counted to us," said Dominic as he looked in Elle's direction and smiled.

"But you got married in your own garden," Sophia reminded him pointedly. "Where we've all gotten married, starting with Mom and Dad."

"Stop it," Matteo said. His arm was around Sophia's shoulders as he leaned down to smile at her. "Let it go, baby. This is not your decision to make."

"I know," Sophia said, sniffling. She gave Ana such a plaintive look that Ana also started crying.

Looking at his daughters, Carlo cried, "*Dio mio,* can we not have a conversation without emotions getting out of hand and tears flowing? We're blessed to be together at Christmas. Let's get some Christmas cheer in here!"

The sisters got up and hugged. "I'm sorry," said Sophia. "I guess I'm still a bit hormonal."

Ana hugged her sister tightly. It was just like her to make a joke out of it. There were no hard feelings. Sophia was outspoken, had always been, and Ana didn't believe that would ever change. However, it was her and Erik's wedding. They would have it as they saw fit.

"I'm not crying because you were rude, which you were. I was crying because I miss your being rude to me to my face instead of on the phone. I've missed you so much!"

"Now this is getting ridiculous," Carlo said. "Dominic and Elle, play something for us, please!"

Dominic and Elle got up and went to the grand piano sitting next to the huge picture window, which displayed the snowy night outside.

Before beginning they whispered something to each other and then Dominic sat down and started playing "Silent Night." Elle sang the operatic version. Her deep contralto tenderly caressed the words and sent them back out at the listeners in rich rounded tones.

Ana reached for Erik's hand as Elle sang and squeezed it reassuringly. His family was also given to emotional outbursts. His grandmother was incorrigible. But she would dub him a saint if he got through the next three days with his sanity intact. She was glad he had such a great sense of humor. Her family took some getting used to.

Erik must have been in tune with her because he leaned down and whispered, "They remind me of my family. I think this is a match made in heaven."

Ana grinned, then, and leaned her head on his shoulder for the rest of the performance. After "Silent Night," Dominic and Elle did a more contemporary song with "Please Come Home for Christmas." Elle belted it out as if she were a soul diva instead of an opera diva and had everyone clapping along. Carlo and Natalie were even inspired to get up and dance.

When she finished the song, Elle went and took Natalie by the hand. "Would you sing "What Child Is This?" I love the way you do it."

Natalie kissed her daughter-in-law on the cheek and said, "It would be my pleasure."

Elle went and sat down and Dominic and his mother took center stage. Natalie was a true soprano and her voice wreaked havoc on the listener's emotions with its sweetness. Although retired from the stage for the most part, she kept her voice in fine shape with daily exercises as was evident in the flawless rendition of the well-known Christmas song about the birth of Christ.

Carlo had tears in his eyes when his wife came back to reclaim her seat beside him. He hugged her, and said, "Thank you, my darling. That was one of Momma's favorites. You got me right here." His hand was over his heart.

Inspired by the other performances, Sophia suddenly grabbed Ana by the hand, saying, "Come on, sis, everyone else has sung a Christmas song. Let's do ours."

Ana looked stricken. "Our song?" she cried incredulously. "You and I don't sing, remember?"

"We did sing a Christmas song, once!" Sophia insisted.

The horror of it, Ana thought. She's talking about the song we did in a Christmas pageant in elementary school. "That song is the reason why *we don't* sing in public," Ana reminded her.

"I don't care," Sophia said. She pointed at Dominic as if to cue him. "'Jingle Bell Rock'!"

"I don't think I know that," Dominic said.

"You're a maestro," said his sister. "Wing it!" She hummed a little to give him the tune.

Laughing, Ana said, "All right, but in English. Last time we did it in Italian and I don't think it translated well."

Dominic winged it, and his sisters sang with gusto if not well. Caterwauling would be a better description of the sound coming out of their mouths. Like two cats fighting in an alley. However, not only did Ana remember the song, but the dance routine Sophia had come up with way back when. They pranced around the room. Their dancing was a whole lot more pleasing than their singing, especially to the men in their lives, because Sophia's choreography called for quite a bit of booty shaking. By the end, they had everyone laughing so hard tears were rolling down their faces. Theirs was the only act that got a standing ovation.

Later, Erik walked Ana to her room door. There was no question that they would not be sharing a room tonight. Ana had merely nodded when her mother had told her that their *rooms* were ready for them. "I hope we didn't wear you out tonight," Ana said almost apologetically as Erik's hand rested gently on her cheek. He bent and planted a kiss on her forehead. "Not at all," he said, "I have all kinds of energy in reserve." His gaze was blatantly sexual.

Ana laughed because she knew he had to be pulling her leg with that look. There was no way she was letting him anywhere near her until they were back in New York City.

"Surely you're kidding," she said, her gaze devouring him just as fervently. He had just set her pulse to racing. Two could play that game. She'd have him *running* to take a cold shower before she was done. "Although I wish I could undress you and tuck you into bed. You've been such a good boy today both with the surprise and keeping your hands to yourself. My parents may even be convinced that we're waiting until our wedding night to make love."

"I was that convincing, huh?" asked Erik. His cheek, which was bristly by this time of night, grazed hers but still the touch turned her on. She had only to turn her head a fraction of an inch and their mouths would meet in a longed-for kiss. She hadn't kissed him since they had arrived hours ago and that one had been interrupted by her dad.

"Oh, hell, I give up. Just kiss me and kiss me hard so I can go take a cold shower!" she said, frustrated. Erik grinned and went in for the kill. They had shared many kisses since their first kiss, but this one was special because it was somehow forbidden. He felt like a schoolboy stealing kisses and although this scenario should not be the least bit sensual to a grown man, it was.

The kiss deepened and, honestly, if not for the sound of footsteps on the hardwood floor behind them they would have continued for some time. However, the footsteps were followed by a deep voice with an Italian accent saying, *"Buona notte,* Ana!"

It was said with authority and finality. Unlike Erik, Ana knew that when her father said *"Buona notte,"* he only said it when the person he was speaking to was going directly to bed, no detours. That's all he had to say to them when they were children and they knew not to talk back.

"Buona notte, Papa," said Ana. *"Ti amo,"* she whispered to Erik.

"I love you," Erik whispered back.

Ana gave him one last glance and went into her room.

Erik turned to face Carlo. "Good night, sir."

Carlo laughed softly. "Good night? It's still early. There's something I'd like to talk with you about."

Concern was mirrored in Erik's eyes as he regarded Carlo. "Lead the way."

They went into the study, a masculine room with book-lined walls and leather furnishings. There was a bar in a corner of the room and Carlo went and poured them both shots of brandy.

"Only a little," Erik said. "I'm not much of a drinker."

Sometimes he hated admitting that because he knew that some men judged other men on their ability to hold their liquor. If he were to be judged on that basis, he'd fail miserably.

"Good for you," said Carlo. "I've seen the love of a drink ruin many a man."

He prepared them both perhaps half an inch in the tumblers. Handing Erik his drink, he said, "Please sit down."

Erik sat in a dark brown, tufted-leather armchair and Carlo sat in the matching chair opposite him. Carlo took a sip of his brandy before beginning. "What I know of you, I like, Erik. You've worked hard. You sincerely believe in what you do and from what I hear you love your family. But all of that is on the surface. A person is so much more than what shows on the surface. Human beings consist of many layers. Just because a man appears perfect, doesn't mean he is."

"None of us are perfect," Erik said. "I have my faults."

"I'm sure you do," said Carlo. "So have I. What I'm getting at is I don't want my daughter marrying a man who is interested only in what he sees. Ana's beautiful, that's a given. Her beauty, however, has been somewhat of a curse. Men are drawn to her because of it, but after a while learn that she's human, not some ideal, and they wind up breaking her heart. I want to make certain that you see more in Ana than what's on the surface. I see the way you look at her. I love my wife more than I did on our wedding day, so I know how you feel about Ana.

But will you love her when she's no longer young? Will you love her after she's given you children and can't lose the baby weight?

Because if the answer is no, I wish you would leave her now rather than later."

Erik started to say something and Carlo held up his hand. "I'm not finished. I wasn't going to say this. Earlier I told Ana I had no doubts about you and, truly, my gut tells me you're who you appear to be. But I wouldn't be a good father if I didn't get this off my chest. I've known too many rich men who married beautiful women and tossed them aside when a more beautiful woman came along."

Erik drank some of the brandy and grimaced. It was quality brandy, but it still burned going down. He simply had no tolerance for alcohol. He looked Carlo straight in the eye. "I don't make decisions lightly and I would never have proposed to Ana if I wasn't sure she's the woman I want to spend the rest of my life with."

He went on to tell Carlo about his mother and how he had been a grown man before he'd come to terms with her behavior toward his father and him and Belana. "I'm thirty-five, and Ana is the only woman I've ever loved because she is the only woman I ever trusted enough to allow to get close to me. And that wouldn't have happened if I hadn't followed the advice of my sister who told me to be Ana's friend, just her friend, for as long as she wanted me to be. It's true. I was smitten with Ana from the start. A fool in love, but spending time with her without having any romantic expectations gave me a good look into her soul. Yes, Mr. Corelli, I love Ana for much more than her appearance. I love that she's smart, she's kind to others. She adores her friends and family. And there's no truer friend than your daughter. Does that answer your question?"

Carlo smiled and nodded in the affirmative. "I'm satisfied," he said. He set his empty glass on the side table next to the lamp where he was sitting and got to his feet. Erik set his nearly untouched drink down, too, and stood. They shook hands, which felt like Carlo's seal of approval to Erik. "Welcome to the family, son," said Carlo. Then he hugged Erik briefly and added, *"Buono notte."* With that he turned and left the room.

Erik went to bed. When he got to his room he dialed Ana's cell phone number.

"Hello, darling," Ana said, her voice husky.

"I think I just had 'the talk' with your father," Erik said, laughter evident in his tone.

"It had to happen sooner or later," Ana told him. "He's a traditionalist. What did he say?"

"He just wanted to know that I'm sincere," Erik said, "and I assured him I was. Could we have all boys when we have children? I don't know if I can be a father to a girl. It's too complicated."

Ana laughed. "You'll have to talk to God about that."

"I'll do that when I say my prayers tonight. Right after I thank Him for you."

"Okay, darling, sleep well," Ana said, laughing softly. "I'll dream about you."

* * *

The following day was Christmas Eve, Ana and Erik were the first ones up since they had been designated to prepare breakfast. It was a bright day, the sunlight reflecting off the snowbanks outside. Per the rental agreement someone had come that morning to shovel the snow from the walkway in front of the house and the snow plow had been in the neighborhood as well, so the roads were clear. After breakfast the men went to buy a Christmas tree and the women, with the children, made the kitchen their gathering place as Elle and Natalie, along with help from Ana, began cooking Christmas dinner. Tomorrow no one planned to be slaving over a hot stove while they could be spending time with the family.

Sophia happily took charge of the children, keeping the girls entertained with games and coloring books and the babies were content to be in their carriers with cheerful sounds all around them.

Ana had to smile because her mother clearly deferred to Elle when it came to recipes. Elle listed items and Natalie followed orders as if she were Elle's sous chef and without attitude. She was not a diva in the kitchen.

The turkey and ham were in the oven. Elle was washing turnip greens in the sink and Natalie was stirring the macaroni and cheese in a pot on the stove top prior to putting it into the oven. Sophia had put on a CD of Christmas music to which they hummed.

"This reminds me of when my grandmother and I would cook together," Elle said, smiling at the thought.

"It was a lot of work but the end results were always worth it."

"I hope so," said Ana, struggling with the pecan pie she was making. She thought the mixture looked too watery but Elle assured her that the pie would firm up when it had finished baking. Ana went and put the pie in one of the double ovens. She peeked at the panettone while she had the oven door open. The dough had risen ten hours, after which Carlo had punched it down in its bowl and then transferred the dough to two baking pans and allowed the dough to rise five more hours. Her father had said the two loaves should cook for approximately forty-five minutes. No wonder most people in Milan buy their panettone from a reputable baker, Ana thought.

The conquering heroes got back around noon with the tree, an eight-foot fir. Famished, they were served hot soup and grilled cheese sandwiches for lunch. After which the women insisted they put the tree up so it could be decorated.

That night, after dinner, the family put the finishing touches on the tree and it took pride of place in front of the picture window in the entertainment room not far from the grand piano. Presents were put under the tree as well as the panettone which was carefully wrapped by Carlo. Ariana and Renata took particular delight in the tree-lighting ceremony. Ariana, with the help of her father, got to put the star at the top of the tree, and Renata with the help of *her* father got to switch on the lights.

The babies had been put to bed earlier in the evening. At around nine o'clock Carlo sternly told Ariana and Renata, "You must go to bed now, girls, or else *Babbo Natale* will not bring you any presents."

Ariana and Renata looked at each other with stretched eyes. They believed every word out of their grandfather's mouth. With urgency they began kissing everyone good-night and hurried their parents along so they could be tucked into bed as quickly as possible and go fast asleep for fear of angering *Babbo Natale*.

Once the girls were off to bed and there was no chance of them hearing, Natalie exclaimed, "You get a kick out of scaring those sweet babies, don't you?"

Her husband laughed quietly. "That's half the fun, *cara mia*."

On Christmas morning, Ana was awakened by the sound of her nieces' high-pitched screams of delight. *Babbo Natale* had apparently visited during the night and left them presents. She hurried into the nearby bathroom to wash her face and brush her teeth, then put on a bathrobe and slippers and joined her family around the Christmas tree.

Everyone was there, also in robes and slippers. The mothers held their sons and the fathers their daughters in their laps as the little girls tore the gift wrap off their presents. *"Buon Natale!"* Ana said, smiling.

"Buon Natale," chorused her family back at her.

The adults were not interested in exchanging gifts, only in seeing the joy on the children's faces. This to them was the true meaning of Christmas. After all, it was a child for whom the tradition was started.

Ana sat down beside Erik and he put his arms around her in a warm hug. She kissed his cheek. "Thank you again for doing this for me. I'm so happy!"

"Thank you for loving me," he said in her ear. "That's all the thanks I need."

The following day there were tearful goodbyes at the airport as Ana's family prepared to board the plane for New York City, after which they would take a connecting flight to Italy. She and Erik would also be flying to New York but her family's flight left earlier. She regretted that no one had had the foresight to try to book them all on the same flight.

She kissed them all at the terminal. Her father pulled her and Erik aside for a moment. "Oh, Ana, I forgot to tell you, Pietro Lanza is heading up the New York office. He's already in New York but is staying at a hotel until he can find more permanent accommodations. I gave him your number. He doesn't know anyone in the city."

"I didn't know Pietro had been promoted," said Ana. "Good for him."

"Yes," said her father. "He's earned it."

"It'll be nice to see your first love again, huh?" Sophia said, interrupting with a mischievous grin on her face. She looked at Erik. "Oh, she was wild about him."

Ana laughed. "We were twelve!"

"I don't care, you never forget your first love," Sophia teased.

It was announced that passengers could begin boarding the plane. Ana got in a few additional kisses, and she and Erik waved goodbye to her family.

Chapter 11

Natalie phoned Ana to let her know they had arrived home safely. Ana was snuggling in bed with Erik, his body pressed close to hers. He slept soundly while she talked.

The subject returned to wedding plans. "Your sister's heart was in the right place," Natalie said in her older daughter's defense. "You do need to start thinking seriously about what you want to do. Do you want a winter wedding or a spring wedding? Call me when you decide. As your mother, I do want to be involved."

"All right, Mom, I'll call you," Ana promised.

Natalie was unable to suppress a yawn. "I could sleep for a week. Your father's already snoring. I'd better go. Take care, sweetheart."

"You, too," said Ana. Ana hung up the phone and got comfortable in Erik's arms once more.

He stirred. "Your folks?"

"Yeah," she murmured. "Letting me know they're home. Are you awake or talking in your sleep?"

He kissed her naked shoulder. "I'm awake."

Ana felt him hardening. "Awake enough to discuss the wedding?"

"Okay," he said, sounding disappointed to her.

"You keep telling me to do what I like, but what about your schedule? Would work get in the way of a honeymoon if we were married during a certain time of year?"

"You're asking if I have a busy time of the year?" he asked.

"Well, yeah."

"I can arrange time off at any time you prefer," he told her.

"Really, Erik, you're too flexible."

He kissed the back of her neck. "I'll show you flexible."

She squirmed in his arms. "You're no help at all."

He cupped her left breast. "Let's get married in June. I hear June weddings are nice."

"Then you want to be married outdoors?"

"Yes, you choose the place."

"Your parents' garden in New Haven," she said. "I want Drusilla there and travel isn't easy on her, even though she'd deny it."

"I'm sure Mom and Dad and Grandma would love that," Erik said.

"Okay, that's settled," Ana said smiling, "How many guests?"

"Oh, a few hundred," Erik joked.

"Be serious. Family and close friends only," Ana said with a tired sigh. "The guest list is always longer in the end than when it starts out. Let's say a hundred, tops."

"That's fine," Erik said. "And I hope the paparazzi will leave you alone."

Ana hadn't thought about that. She didn't know why. She'd seen scenes where the paparazzi were camped out at wedding venues of celebrities hoping to get that money shot—that spectacular photo that would sell for an outrageous amount.

"We won't put the announcement in the papers," she suggested. "No one has to know except those who get invitations."

"And you expect everyone to keep our secret?" he asked skeptically.

"I know I'm being unrealistic, but we can try it," Ana returned.

Ana touched his cheek. He smiled. "Your eyes are the color of the sunset over the ocean in Tahiti," she said.

"You would know," he said.

"Yes," she said, grinning. She gently kissed his lips. "And your lips are soft as a feather from heaven."

"How poetic," he whispered with a naughty glint in

his eye. "Have you been in contact with many feathers from heaven lately?" His hands were squeezing her butt.

"I don't think you know your sexual appeal," she continued, ignoring for the moment the ache in her feminine core. "Women come on to you all the time and you don't even notice."

"I notice, I just don't care," Erik said truthfully. His penis was fully erect now. He rolled over and got a condom off the nightstand's top where he had tossed a couple a few hours ago. Handing it to Ana, he said, "Would you?"

Ana took it, tore it open and easily rolled the latex condom onto him. The wrapper was dropped onto the nightstand and she climbed on top of him. Her hair spilled down her back. Erik enjoyed the sight of her, full breasts with the nipples erect and pointing north. Her skin felt soft as silk beneath his fingers. He went deep inside her and felt her contract around his shaft. Felt the need building within her. She wasn't shy anymore.

She was now comfortable enough to tell him what she wanted, and bold enough to take it. Her breasts bounced up and down as they increased their efforts. She grasped his hands, their fingers entwined, soft pants issuing from her full lips. Sometimes they made love but sometimes they carried on like a pair of animals in the wild. This was one of those times. She closed her eyes and he knew she was about to scream when he felt her tremble inside. She screamed and fell on top of him. He came in a powerful rush, so turned on by her taking her pleasure that he could no longer hold on to his. As he collapsed back onto the bed she was smiling with satisfaction. He pushed the hair out of her eyes and wrapped his strong arms around her and then, worried she might catch a chill, he pulled the covers up over them.

Ana lay there thinking that if she had never gotten up the nerve to tell Erik how she really felt about him, she would be in this bed alone, except perhaps for a book by one of her favorite authors. Things had certainly changed.

To thank her for arranging the Aspen trip Ana sent Abby flowers and a gift certificate for the works at an exclusive spa. She knew from a past conversation with Abby that she longed for a day of pampering, however considered an expensive spa too much of a splurge. Her husband was a schoolteacher, after all. Ana got Erik to agree to give Abby the day off. Abby would have no feasible reason to refuse Ana's gift.

When Pietro Lanza phoned Ana a couple of days before New Year's Eve, she wasn't at all surprised. But she was a bit at a loss for words. She hadn't seen him or spoken to him since they were twelve and he and his widowed mother, Maria, moved to Rome. Ana's mother and Maria Lanza were friends and had stayed in touch, so when Pietro decided to work in the fashion industry he had been hired by Ana's father and moved back to Milan. Every now and then her father would mention that Pietro was doing well and swiftly climbing the corporate ladder. It was Sophia who had trained him and now Pietro had been given a position, which would have been hers if she had not wanted to remain in Milan. But she preferred raising her children in her hometown.

Ana didn't even recognize Pietro's voice, which was deep and sexy. They naturally lapsed into Italian as soon as he introduced himself and after ten minutes or so, Ana relaxed and remembered how comfortable she used to be around him. "You must come to the Whitaker's New Year's Eve party," she said. "I'd love to see you."

"I don't know," he hesitated. "I don't have a date."

"Come solo," Ana suggested. "You'll probably meet someone at the party."

"You always were an optimist," he said, laughter evident in his voice.

"Then you'll come?"

"Yes, I'll be there," he agreed.

The Whitaker's New Year's Eve party was an opportunity to dress to the nines and toast in the New Year with people you admired. Erik and Ana greeted guests as they began arriving at nine. She wore a short, sleeveless scoop-neck silver matte dress with black accessories. Erik wore a black tuxedo with a red bow tie and white cummerbund.

Music played softly in the background. The band wouldn't begin their first set until ten.

Guests mingled and partook of the feast at the buffet tables and imbibed spirits offered up by bars at either end of the room. The penthouse was huge with plenty of space to accommodate the expected one hundred-plus revelers.

The hardwood floors were ideal for dancing and the view of the New York City skyline was awe-inspiring in daylight but even more so at night.

Ana could not restrain herself when Abby arrived with her husband, Harry. She walked swiftly to the older woman and hugged her. "Wow, you look fantastic!"

Abby had abandoned her smooth chignon in favor of a wavy, chin length style that accentuated her high cheekbones and beautifully framed her heart-shaped face. She wore a sleeveless black dress with a square-shaped bodice and sparkly silver sandals with a matching clutch. Her fake fur sable coat was the same color as her hair, a warm auburn. Harry looked wonderful in a black tuxedo with white tie and white cummerbund. While his wife was petite, he was tall and lanky, his head completely bald. He reminded Ana of a young James Earl Jones, especially when he smiled and she saw a small gap between his teeth.

"I had a ball at the spa," Abby said, her eyes twinkling. She peered down at her feet and wiggled her toes. "Look, passionate pink."

"Fabulous!" Ana declared, admiring the color. They giggled together like little girls.

Meanwhile, Erik and Harry were shaking hands and murmuring masculine hellos. Harry glanced at Abby and Ana, a smile on his face. "How did we get so lucky?"

Erik laughed shortly. "Beats me," he said. Indeed,

both Ana and Abby were radiant tonight but it was not due to what they were wearing but to how content they seemed to be with their lives. Erik had always admired Harry and Abby for their devotion to one another. He wished for himself and Ana to enjoy such a long and happy marriage.

Abby came and grabbed Harry by the hand. "I'm starving."

Harry peered over his shoulder at Erik and Ana as he let himself be lead away by his wife. "She's been eating like a bird, afraid she wouldn't fit in that dress."

Ana and Erik smiled knowingly. A moment after Abby and Harry left in search of food the bell rang again and Ana opened the door to Pietro and his date, a curvy brunette in a little red dress. Ana recognized Pietro's dark brown, almost black eyes, at once. Those thick lashes were not easy to forget. Nor his darkly tanned skin, wavy black hair, square jaw and full-lipped mouth. He had been a beautiful boy and he was a gorgeous man.

"Ana!" he exclaimed and pulled her into his arms for a kiss on the mouth—a kiss that, in Erik's estimation, lasted far too long.

Ana was startled for two reasons: she hadn't expected to be kissed on the mouth by Pietro, on the cheek, yes; and she hadn't expected him to show up with a date, especially not a female date.

How had he put it thirteen years ago when she had confessed she liked him, her teenaged heart open and vulnerable? *I like you too, Ana. But, I'm sorry, not in that way. I don't like girls in that way.* His revelation had not been put eloquently but she had certainly understood. Pietro was gay.

"It's a secret," he'd told her in his innocence. "I haven't even told my parents." At the time his father was still living. But a short time after that his father had been killed in a construction accident, and he and his mother had moved to Rome to live with her family.

Ana pulled herself together and introduced Pietro to Erik. "Pietro this is my fiancé, Erik Whitaker. Erik, this is my childhood friend, Pietro Lanza."

The two men shook hands, Erik trying not to let his irritation show on his face.

If he did look irritated, Pietro didn't seem to notice. He enthusiastically pumped Erik's hand. "It's a pleasure to meet you, Erik." He gestured to his date. "I'd like you two to meet Hilary Eastbrook. Hilary is my assistant."

Ana shook Hilary's hand and smiled warmly. "How are you, Hilary?"

Hilary smiled back shyly. "Oh, it's a real treat to meet you, Ms. Corelli. I've followed your career forever!"

Ana continued to smile at the woman who appeared to be about her age, "How sweet," she said. "And, please, call me Ana." Her mind was racing. She knew she couldn't drag Pietro off and interrogate him. He'd just arrived. But she wanted to ask him what had happened to the lovely gay boy she had known thirteen years ago? Had he just been going through a phase? Was that even possible? Of her gay friends, and she had many, once they realized they were gay they didn't suddenly wake up to be heterosexual one morning.

"I happened to mention coming here tonight at the office," Pietro told Ana, "and Hilary started talking about her plans for tonight."

"Which consisted of microwave popcorn and a DVD," joked Hilary.

"So I asked her to join me," Pietro concluded. "Remember, I was reluctant to come without a date."

"I'm glad you asked Hilary," Ana said graciously. The bell rang announcing more guests. "Please, enjoy yourselves."

When Pietro and Hilary were out of earshot, Erik quipped, "He didn't tongue you, did he?"

"Absolutely not," said Ana as they walked to the door. "I wouldn't have let him. Frankly, I'm confused about his behavior."

"Well, I didn't like his behavior, either."

"I don't mean just the kiss," Ana said. She opened the door. Erik's parents and Drusilla had arrived. Pietro was forgotten as she and Erik welcomed them. A short time later, Belana and Nick showed up, looking wonderful in their evening clothes. They were the last of the guests on the list, so Erik and Ana went to stand in the middle of the dance floor to formally welcome everyone and introduce the band.

The local five-member blues band included a pianist, two guitar players, a drummer and a trumpet player. Their vocalist, who simply called herself Maybelline, was an attractive full-figured African-American woman

with a powerful voice. She went right into an upbeat set
that got the guests onto the dance floor. Erik and Ana
set the example by being the first couple on the floor,
followed by Belana and Nick.

Maybelline sang, "Something's Got a Hold on Me,"
with verve. It was lively enough to lend itself to a swing
dance which is what Erik and Ana wound up doing to
the delight of the guests. Not to be outdone Belana and
Nick displayed their talent for the intricate twists and
turns in that style of dance. At one point the couples'
movements brought them close enough to converse on
the dance floor and Ana called to Belana. "It's not fair.
You're a professional."

"All's fair in love and dance," Belana joked, and allowed Nick to lift her in the air.

"I hope you don't want to try that," Erik said, laughing.

"And break my neck?" Ana replied, admiring Belana
and Nick's skill. "No, thank you," she joked.

After two more songs, which were designed to get
the party started, Maybelline slowed things down a bit
with "This Magic Moment." Ana felt a gentle tap on her
shoulder. She turned around to find Drusilla standing
behind her. "May I have this dance with my grandson?"

Ana relinquished her dance partner after kissing
Drusilla's cheek, and saying, "Don't wear him out."

"I can't make any promises," was Drusilla's cheeky
response.

Because Drusilla was so short, Erik had to bend
down a bit to dance with his grandmother. He felt like

picking her up and setting her on the tops of his feet like he'd seen some fathers do with their little girls at weddings.

Drusilla gazed up at him through her thick glasses. "You're devilishly handsome tonight. You remind me of your grandfather when we first got married. We used to dance the night away at the Savoy in Harlem."

Ana was not without a dance partner for long. Pietro claimed her. She took the opportunity to catch up on as much as they could of the last thirteen years as they danced.

"Why didn't you answer any of my letters?" she asked, peering into his eyes.

"We were still grieving when we left Milan. Everything had changed overnight, it seemed. My mother cried all the time. I thankfully read your letters but didn't know how to respond. I had told you something I'd never shared with anyone else. I was scared I had done the wrong thing. And months later after I'd also told my mother, I knew I had to stop telling people about my true feelings. I thought it best to sever ties with anyone who knew the truth."

"She didn't take it well?" asked Ana, concerned.

"Not at all," Pietro confirmed. His expression was sad as he continued, "Her husband was dead and now her son was gay? She told me she had a heart condition and I shouldn't be joking about something that outrageous. I followed her cue and told her I'd been teasing and never brought it up again."

"Does she really have a heart condition?"

"I've never seen any medical records, but I doubt it."

"So you keep your private life private," Ana deduced.

"Unfortunately, yes," he said softly, smiling at her. "In all fairness I could have made things clear to her years ago, but even today it's easier to be considered hetero than it is to be outwardly gay. It isn't easy leading a double life. Women take it I'm an Italian stallion because of the way I look. And any serious relationship I attempt with a man ends badly because I won't declare to the world that I want to be with him. So I don't have anyone special in my life."

His explanation had the ring of truth to Ana. The recent glut of news stories about bullying and young gay people committing suicide because of continual mistreatment proved that it was still not safe to be yourself in today's society.

She hugged him. "You're still so young. You'll find someone. In the meantime, your secret's safe with me."

He sighed with relief. "I'm glad you're the same old Ana, the one I could always talk to."

They once again regained the proper distance and continued the dance. When the song ended, Pietro asked Hilary to dance, and Ana returned to Erik's arms.

"You looked kind of cozy with Pietro," Erik commented dryly.

"We were just talking," Ana said nonchalantly. "He's had a hard time finding someone he can relate to. We always found it easy to talk to each other." She moved closer to him and laid her head on his shoulder. "Don't worry, sweetie, I'm not his type."

"I'm not worried," Erik denied.

"You sounded a little put out."

"I get antsy when another man touches my girl."

She smiled up at him. "Rest assured, your girl would not allow anyone to touch her inappropriately. Italians are bit more demonstrative than Americans, that's all. When we see friends and family we kiss, we hug, we feed them." She ended with a laugh.

"You could also be describing African-Americans," Erik said with a grin. He gestured to the buffet table in the distance where Abby was feeding Harry a jumbo shrimp.

It was nearing the midnight hour when Ana went into the store room to retrieve the party hats and noisemakers. Everyone helped themselves from the huge box and then Erik directed their attention to the big screen TV that had been installed on the wall above the fireplace in the great room.

Champagne glasses were filled and then everyone was ready for the countdown. Couples put their arms around one another. When the ball dropped in Times Square everyone at the Whitaker's New Year's Eve party shouted, "Happy New Year!"

Erik and Ana kissed as did every other couple in the room. The band struck up "Auld Lang Syne" and those who remembered the words sang along. Laughter abounded, but some tears were shed, too.

"This year will be the best ever," Erik whispered in Ana's ear, "Because I'm marrying you."

Ana just smiled and kissed him again.

Chapter 12

"Eat, eat," Pietro encouraged Ana, stuffing pizza into his own mouth.

Laughing, Ana purposely put down the pizza slice in her hand. "What? Do you have orders to fatten me up or something?"

"You're representing a line of clothing designed for full-figured women and you're too skinny," Pietro complained good-naturedly.

"I'm not one of those size-zero models. I'm a size eight, I'm not skinny. Anyway, that's why you're using models of all sizes in the ads, so no woman will feel left out." She picked up the pizza again. "Now, let me eat in peace!"

They dined at a pizzeria not far from the studio of Ivan Ivanovich, the world-renowned photographer, where Ana had posed for him in the new line of clothes. The shoot had lasted for ten hours. Ana was worn out and not very hungry but she'd agreed to a pizza with Pietro after the shoot because Erik was out of town. She was used to his frequent business trips and had vowed not to become a nagging fiancée. Though she missed him terribly.

It was now the last week in January and she and Pietro had been working hard to put the finishing touches on the spring campaign for Voluptuous Woman, Corelli Fashions' full-figured line.

She was enjoying getting to know Pietro all over again. The boy she had loved was still in there. He was sweet, and kind and funny. She found herself wanting to find a guy for him. Matchmaking wasn't something she usually considered, believing that sticking your nose in someone else's love life rarely ended well. In spite of her misgivings, though, whenever she ran into male gay friends she made it a point to ask if they were presently involved with anyone.

She looked at Pietro now, "Are you still seeing Hilary?"

"We're friends," he said, but she could tell by his reluctance to meet her gaze he wasn't being completely truthful. Pietro was a bad liar.

"Does she know that?"

"Nothing's going to happen between us," he said, raising his gaze to hers. "I never get intimate with women. I break up with them before it gets to that stage."

"Isn't it going to be difficult to break up with Hilary since she's your assistant?" Ana asked pointedly. She hated to see him squirm but someone had to ask him the hard questions.

He sighed. "You're right. I should tell her we can't date anymore."

"Good luck with that," Ana said. "She's already half in love with you."

He shook his head. "She just has a little crush."

"Have you ever seen yourself in a mirror? You're better looking than most male models. You can't casually date women. One of these days you're going to run into a nut who won't take no for an answer."

"Been there," he admitted. "I've been stalked a few times."

"See? It's not nice to play with women's emotions," Ana said, reaching over to grasp his hand. She met his gaze, her expression serious. "How do you know your mother doesn't already know and accept your sexuality? Many of my gay friends have said that when they told their parents they already were aware they were gay. Kind of a letdown, isn't it? I mean you get all prepared for an emotional scene and your mom looks at you and says, 'Yeah, I've known that for a long time now.' Of course *you'll* never find out unless you talk to her."

"I know, I know," said Pietro, his eyes downcast.

"That's the end of my speech," said Ana. "I won't bring it up again, ever. I just hate to see you so unhappy."

"I'm getting there," Pietro said. "One day soon I'm going to tell her, and let it hit the fan."

Ana didn't comment. She felt she had harangued him enough. It was his life, therefore it was his decision.

"What I'd rather be talking about is how you and Ivan were looking at each other," she teased lightly. "He's available, you know. His longtime boyfriend was killed in a car accident about two years ago and he's been taking things slowly when it comes to romance. It's hard when you lose someone you love like that. But he recently told me he's thinking of dating again. If you're interested I could put in a good word for you."

Pietro colored. Ana smiled because she had obviously judged Ivan and Pietro's encounter correctly—Pietro was interested in the sexy photographer.

"He wouldn't be interested in me," Pietro said. "He's famous. I'm just a worker bee."

"You're the head of the New York office of an international company," Ana said enthusiastically. "I'm not gonna let you down-rate yourself."

Pietro scrunched up his face. "Do you really think he's interested? He's gorgeous. He reminds me of that guy who's in that vampire show on HBO."

"Alexander Skarsgard." Ana supplied the name of the handsome actor.

"Yeah, him," Pietro murmured wistfully. "I don't know, Ana."

"Faint heart never won fair…um, guy," Ana said encouragingly.

"I'll think about it," Pietro said noncommittally.

"Okay, cool," Ana relented. "But don't think too long. A guy like Ivan won't be on the market forever."

They finished the pizza, and when they left the restaurant it was nearly eleven. The wind was fierce and the temperature in the thirties. Nonetheless the streets were crowded in this part of town. Ana momentarily gazed up at the night sky. There were too many tall buildings obscuring her view of the heavens to tell if there were any stars out. When they were in Aspen one of the things she'd liked most was walking out at night and seeing the sky lit up with stars twinkling like diamonds.

"I'll take you home," said Pietro, putting her arm through his in a gentlemanly fashion.

"You live farther away than I do," Ana said reasonably. "I can get home on my own."

"I insist."

"All right," Ana relented, touched by his gesture.

Half an hour later they were walking into her loft. Ana shut and locked the door behind them, then turned to Pietro and said, "Look, why don't you just stay here tonight? I've plenty of room. It's Friday, you don't have to be at the office in the morning."

"You had to remind me," said Pietro as he walked into the living room and picked up the TV's remote and switched it on. "Friday night, and I don't have a date."

"I'm sure Hilary would have gone out with you if you hadn't had to work late," Ana said teasingly.

"I mean a real date."

Ana pulled off her jacket revealing jeans and a long-sleeve black pullover sweater. "So I take it that you're staying. Hand me your coat."

Pietro pulled off his zippered black leather coat and handed it to Ana. "You convinced me. What sort of movies do you have? Got any popcorn?"

Chuckling, Ana put their coats in the foyer closet and joined him in the living room. "Let's see, I just got *Ninja Assassin*, have you seen it?" She knew of Pietro's predilection for martial arts movies. Or, at least, he used to like them. They used to argue about who the best martial arts actor was. She liked Jackie Chan because he was also funny. Pietro preferred Jet Li because, in Pietro's words, he was such a badass.

"Seen it?" he said, his eyes lighting up. "About ten times. Put it on."

Ana did so, and then she went to the kitchen to microwave some popcorn. When she returned with the bowl of popcorn and two sodas, Pietro was fast-forwarding through the previews on the DVD.

"Hold on, I like watching those," she protested. "I might see something I'm interested in seeing."

Pietro laughed. "I knew people like you existed, but I just had never met one before. You actually have the patience to watch the previews and not want to get right to the movie?"

Ana set the bowl of popcorn on the coffee table in front of them and handed him a Coke. Her eyes were on the TV's screen. "Another *Nightmare on Elm Street* movie," she said. "Glad I missed that one. Freddy Krueger never dies."

She sat down beside him on the couch. Finally the movie's selection screen came on, and Ana grimaced. "This already looks like it's going to be bloody." The photo was of Rain, the star of the film, dressed in black leather with a chain whipped across his body a deadly blade at its tip, cuts over all of him and his mouth open in what looked like a war cry.

Pietro smiled. "It's not so bad." He pressed play.

The first ten minutes was a bloodbath. Ana watched only through slits of her eyelids. "Oh, my God, tell me when it's over!"

But then Naomie Harris came onto the screen portraying an investigator for Europol trying to prove that Ninjas existed and were hired assassins and the movie became more enjoyable.

Because she was exhausted Ana wound up going to sleep halfway through. Pietro finished watching the movie, then got up to go to the bathroom. When he returned to the living room, Erik was entering into the loft having used his key.

The expression on Erik's face froze Pietro in his footsteps. The muscles worked in Erik's strong jaw. His eyes narrowed. "I had no idea you would be here," he said coldly.

Erik had not yet seen Ana asleep on the couch because the couch's back was to the front door of the loft. He would've had to enter the living room to see her laying there.

"Ana and I worked late, I saw her home, and since I live quite a distance away she suggested I stay the night on the couch," Pietro told him in a low voice. Adding the couch part had seemed like a prudent choice. "I'm sorry but Ana didn't tell me she was expecting you."

"I was going to surprise her," Erik said. *And what's it to you?* "Where *is* Ana?" He knew he shouldn't be allowing his mind to take him to this dark place but seeing Pietro there at this late of an hour had brought out the jealous fool in him. And why was Pietro whispering?

Pietro gestured to the couch. Erik walked around and saw Ana. She was sleeping peacefully. He looked around the room. An empty bowl with a few popcorn kernels in it was on the coffee table, two soda cans beside it. Ana was fully clothed. So was Pietro. There was no evidence that anything of a sexual nature had happened here and, yet, he felt like he had walked in on Ana and Pietro and caught them red-handed.

He had to get hold of himself. He turned and began walking toward the door. He couldn't let Ana see him this way. Pietro started to say something but when he saw the tightly wound tension in Erik's face he thought better of it. "I'm going," Erik said to Pietro. "Don't tell Ana I was here."

Pietro let him go, but as soon as the door closed behind Erik, he hastily typed out a text message to Ana, explaining that he'd decided to go home after all. He grabbed his coat from the foyer closet, put it on and left.

He caught up with Erik out on the street. "Erik, wait!"

Erik stopped walking, but his face was still a mask

of anger when he turned toward Pietro. Pietro couldn't tell if the anger was directed at him or perhaps was the result of Erik waging a war within himself. It didn't matter. He needed to talk to Erik now.

However, before he could say a word, Erik said, "Don't try to tell me you don't love Ana because I've seen the way you look at her!"

"I've known Ana longer than I've known anyone else in this world besides my mother," Pietro began. "We played together as babies. We lost touch but now that I've found her, I don't ever want to let that happen again. I hope you and I can be friends. But if that's asking too much, I understand. Just know this, I do love her but not in the way you must imagine I do. I love her like a sister."

Erik laughed mockingly. "A man cannot love Ana like a sister unless he is her brother and you're not related to her by blood."

"Ana tells me you two were friends before you fell in love," Pietro said hopefully.

"Ana didn't tell you the whole truth. We were attracted to each other from the beginning. We used restraint."

"You think I'm biding my time until Ana realizes it's me she loves and she leaves you for me?" Pietro asked. He couldn't hide the disbelief in his voice.

"Look," said Erik. "I trust Ana. I know she wouldn't cheat on me. But I don't know you. Therefore, I don't trust you."

"Would you believe me if I told you that Ana isn't even my type?"

"No," said Erik flatly.

"Then I suppose I should save my breath," said Pietro. He sighed heavily. "It's obvious nothing's going to be resolved tonight. I'm going home. I suggest you go back upstairs and surprise Ana. She misses you. I sent her a text message telling her I went home. But if you want to bite off your nose to spite your face, go right ahead."

Pietro walked off. Damn Erik Whitaker! The lucky bastard had one of the best women in the world and he was going to mess it up with his jealous nature. Sure, he realized he could clear things up in seconds by telling Erik he was gay, but why should he? If Erik didn't trust Ana to stay faithful to him, he didn't deserve her! He wished he had someone in his life who loved *him* as much as Ana loved Erik.

Erik stood a moment on the sidewalk, indecision eating at him. He wanted to go back upstairs to Ana but he was still in a rotten mood. He didn't want to subject her to what might spill forth from his mouth while he was fighting to subdue his baser nature. He was only a man, a man with unresolved abandonment issues, if he wasn't mistaken about the gut-wrenching emotion that filled him when he walked in the door and found Pietro standing there.

He was afraid of losing Ana. That was the reason he had left. If she found out that for one split second he had thought her capable of cheating on him she would conclude that maybe they'd gotten engaged too quickly and would call the wedding off. He needed time to cool off.

So he went home.

A persistent beeping woke Ana. She raised herself on her elbow enough to reach her cell phone atop the coffee table. It was a message from Pietro. She sat up more and looked around her. "Pietro?" No answer. She read the message then knew that she was alone in the loft. He must have had something important to do at his place she surmised. She got up, collected the bowl and the empty drink cans and took them into the kitchen.

Once she'd washed the popcorn bowl and put the cans in the recycling bin, she glanced up at the clock. It was nearly two-thirty. She thought of Erik, alone in his hotel room in San Francisco. Should she phone him? What time was it out there? Three hours earlier, right? That made it only eleven thirty.

She went and got her cell phone and dialed his number. Curiously, it went straight to message. "Sweetie, I just wanted to hear your voice before going to bed. Pietro and I worked late on the spring campaign and then he insisted on seeing that I got home safely. He's such a gentleman. I told him to just stay over, it was so late. We started watching a movie and I fell asleep and when I woke up he was gone. I guess I snored." She ended with a laugh. "I love you! Call me when you get this. I don't care how late it is." Shortly after leaving the message, Ana drifted off to sleep again.

She woke up the next morning refreshed and ready

to take on her day. She had no plans to work with Pietro on the campaign today but first she had an appointment with a well-known actress whose portrait she had agreed to paint. That wasn't until eleven. It was now 8:28. She got up and showered.

Her cell phone rang as she was pouring herself a cup of coffee twenty minutes later. She grinned when she saw that it was Erik. "Good morning, my love," she said, her tone husky. "I hope you're home."

"I'm home," Erik confirmed. She could hear the smile in his voice. "I can't wait to see you."

"Then come on over."

"All right, I will."

He abruptly disconnected.

That was rude, Ana thought, and then she heard his key in the door. All thoughts of his being rude were abandoned as she fairly flew to meet him.

Erik felt like a heel for behaving the way he had last night. He'd spent most of the night lying awake going over and over in his head the reason why he'd reacted that way to Pietro's presence. The thing to do was to tell Ana what had happened with Pietro last night. That's all he could do because he knew now that his reaction had been visceral—he'd had no way of controlling it. It was just there like a physical reaction to being hit in the face, violent and painful.

Now as Ana rained kisses on him, he took her by the arms and set her away from him. "Ana, I've got something to say and I should say it quickly or else I might change my mind."

Ana's big brown eyes were concerned. She stood still and gave him her undivided attention. "What is it? Has something happened? You look sad."

"Let's sit down," he said and walked over to the couch he'd found her sleeping on last night ard sat down. Ana joined him, sitting apart from him because she sensed he needed space this morning.

She was still in her bathrobe. He was wearing his running togs and a zippered jacket which was lined for warmth. His coppery eyes looked into hers. "I came by early this morning at around two and ran into Pietro. I was upset seeing him here. So I left, I didn't want you to see me that way. He followed me out and we argued a bit."

Shock registered on Ana's face but she didn't say anything. He knew her mind was making connections, though. Putting two and two together, probably deducing that Erik was the reason Pietro had gone home. But why hadn't *he* stayed?

He laid it all out for her, telling her exactly how he'd felt—like kicking Pietro's ass. Then he told her how vulnerable he had felt at the thought of losing her. And how he thought he had worked through his abandonment issues only to find that he had not. He apologized for allowing such feelings to enter his heart let alone his mind.

Ana listened intently. Her first thought was that she had slept through it all. She hadn't sensed him or smelled his aftershave, nothing. She must have been truly tired. Her second thought was that Pietro had not told Erik he was gay and it therefore was impossible for him to be her lover. Though some gay men have admittedly married and had children, Pietro clearly was not the type to do that. But still it was understandable that Erik would be jealous of all the time she spent with Pietro. Any man would be jealous.

She'd made a promise to Pietro to keep his secret, and that had to be honored even if she *wanted* to tell Erik to ease his mind. She was in a quandary. Should her loyalty be to a friend who had told her something in confidence thirteen years ago? Or to the man she loved to help him feel secure?

She took Erik's hands in hers and maintained eye contact. "You had every right to feel the way you did. I would have been livid if I'd walked in and a beautiful woman was in your house. A woman you'd had a prior relationship with, even though it was a friendly relationship. But Pietro and I aren't even attracted to each other."

Erik slowly shook his head in the negative. "I have the feeling you're not being totally honest with me. It seems as though you're holding something back."

Ana lowered her gaze only for a second or two, but Erik caught the guilty expression in her eyes and that was all it took for him to declare, "Ana, I came here because I felt guilty for my accusatory reaction last night. I wanted to tell you how I felt and apologize for feeling that way. I even considered apologizing to Pietro because, frankly, I think I scared the guy last night. Now I'm sensing some kind of subterfuge."

Ana's guilty conscience made her defensive. "Why can't you just trust that I'm not going to be unfaithful to you? Shouldn't that be enough? I trust *you!*"

"And I trust you," Erik returned evenly. Although as he stood, his jaw set stubbornly, and looked down at her. Ana could swear he didn't even like her very much at that moment, let alone trust her. "I have to go. It was a mistake coming back here so soon. I'm still angry and I don't want to say something I'll regret."

Ana stood, too, pulling her bathrobe tightly around her as if she didn't want to reveal too much of herself to Erik Whitaker. She felt wounded. His words cut like a knife. "Yes, you'd better go," she said, hurt. "I have nothing more to say. You either trust me or you don't. And you don't."

Erik simply looked at her, a frown knitting his brows together. What he wanted to say to her at that moment left a bitter taste in his mouth so he thought it wise not to voice the words. Why was she putting a childhood friend before him? He felt betrayed.

Ana met his gaze. She'd already looked away once and he'd taken that as a sign of guilt. She realized that she was nervously twisting the engagement ring around and around on her finger. Should she give it back to him? No, she thought. This was only the first argument they'd ever had. Surely this was not the end of them.

Erik broke eye contact with her and walked out, leaving her to close the door.

She stood with her back pressed against the closed door, willing herself not to cry. This was nothing. It would blow over as soon as Erik found out Pietro posed no threat to him. But then, it occurred to her that Pietro was not really the problem here. The problem was... Erik didn't trust her.

Chapter 13

Business kept Erik from stewing in his own juices the next few days. He thought about Ana, but he didn't have time to obsess over the situation. Like many businesses Whitaker Enterprises had taken a financial hit in the past three years but now the economy appeared to be rebounding, and since most of Whitaker Enterprises' interests were in the service industry demand was putting pressure on them to supply enough products to satisfy customers. The first quarter of the year promised to be a very good one. However he did take time to speak with his father about his and Ana's dispute and his father was his usual calm, and reasonable self. "Son, if you'd spent more time dating instead of working you would have known not to say everything that comes to your mind when dealing with women. You might have felt jealous and threatened by Ana's friendship with Pietro but you should have chosen your words more carefully," his father offered.

"Are you saying I shouldn't be completely honest with Ana?"

"No, that's not what I'm saying. I'm saying in any relationship you pick and choose your battles. Was it worth it to put your emotions out there and tell Ana you don't trust her?"

"That's not what I said!"

"When you told her you felt there was something she wasn't telling you," said John, "you were saying you thought she was withholding information and to withhold information is to lie. And if you think she's lying to you, it means you don't think you can trust her."

Erik had sighed over the phone. "That's not what I was trying to get across."

"That's the problem with communicating with the opposite sex. You say one thing, she thinks another. You have to be clear. Don't assume she can read your mind, because she can't. And you can't read hers. Don't leave anything to guesswork."

"It's been a week since we spoke. She won't even return my calls."

"A week, huh?" said his father. "That's not good. At any rate, you shouldn't see her until you're sure you won't project your insecurities onto her. That's what you did, son. I'm sorry to say that your parents weren't the best role models for you. Mari was selfish and I was a workaholic who didn't have one solid relationship with a woman in your formative years. If I hadn't let my hurt force me into an emotional cocoon, you would be better equipped to handle certain situations."

"That's no excuse," Erik insisted. "I'm a man. I should have more control over my behavior."

"Solving a problem takes constant vigilance," his father said. "You've been given your first test. You failed. The next time you'll pass with flying colors."

Erik cringed at the thought of a next time. But he knew there would be one. The way he felt about Ana, fiercely possessive and protective, there would certainly be another time when he would feel threatened and the beast would want to come out and growl at somebody.

"I'll apologize right away," he told his father. "I'll grovel if I have to."

"Oh, now, son, no groveling," said his father jokingly. "Whitaker men don't grovel."

Ana was staying busy, as well. Sometimes she painted until dawn broke. She relished the pleasure good honest work gave her. She had completed the portrait of the actress and since then had accepted a commission to paint the mayor. Also, the publicity person at Corelli Fashions had booked her on several area talk shows to reveal the spring line—she enjoyed doing that. Often the hosts would also mention the fact that she painted and show photos of her work. Subsequently, Damon had been selling her paintings as quickly as she could supply them.

She was a happy girl. Except that she was miserable without Erik. Her mother phoned her late one night when she was painting. She welcomed the interruption because while she was painting the mayor's visage, all she could think about was Erik.

"Darling, something's been on my mind and I'm just going to say it," Natalie said without preamble. "When you told me about Erik being jealous of you and Pietro and how Pietro hurried outside to speak with Erik before he left, I couldn't help wondering why Pietro didn't tell Erik he's gay. That would've diffused the situation in no time."

Ana was momentarily speechless. How did her mother know Pietro was gay?

"You know?" she cried, relief flooding her. If her mother knew there could be only one explanation for her knowledge…Maria Lanza had spoken to her mom about Pietro.

"I've known for years. I never talked about it because Maria says he's still in the closet. She said it seems to her that he started to mention it once when he was a teenager, but he couldn't get it out. Ever since then she's been waiting for him to be a man and come right out and tell her. But he hasn't. You knew?"

"Yeah, he told me when we were kids. He said he did tell her not long after they moved to Rome, but she said she had a heart problem and didn't want to hear something so awful. He didn't want to give her a heart attack so he never brought it up again."

Natalie laughed. "In all the years I've known her Maria has never mentioned having a heart problem. Somebody's not telling the truth. I can see why you wouldn't tell Erik, thinking that you were keeping a secret for a friend. But seeing the trouble he'd inadvertently caused, Pietro should have said something."

Ana didn't want to immediately put the blame on Pietro. "He's been hiding for years. It probably never occurred to him to tell Erik who's basically a stranger to him."

"That's not the point. You're his friend. As far as I know, his oldest friend since Maria and I had play dates for you two practically from birth. He should have done it for *you*."

Ana understood her mother's point of view. A mother fought for her child's happiness. But to allude that Pietro might have had an ulterior motive behind keeping silent was unfair. "No, Mom, the problem isn't Pietro. Erik doesn't trust me."

"Did I ever tell you about the time your father punched a guy in the nose?" Natalie paused. "He and I were dating at the time and the musical director I was working with was a big flirt. The guy made the mistake of commenting on my caboose when we were out to dinner with him and several other people. He'd had too much to drink and said I had the nicest ass he'd ever seen. Your father punched his lights out right at the dinner table. The waiter had to revive him by throwing a pitcher of water in his face. You're lucky Erik is not a violent man, like your father! And your father's attitude had nothing to do with not trusting me. He simply acted on impulse. It's not that Erik doesn't trust you. It's his possessiveness he has to curb."

"He never acted possessive before we got engaged," Ana pointed out.

"You never gave him reason to behave that way," her mother also pointed out. "Did you?"

"No," Ana admitted softly.

"Stop pouting and answer his calls," her mother advised.

"I will," Ana said. However, she had another idea. Implementing that idea would solve two problems at once. That is if, indeed, her mother was right about Pietro's behaving selfishly.

She ran the idea by her mother, who said, "Go for it!"

Ana put the first part of her plan in action the very next day. It was a Monday and she was scheduled to go over the final photographs Ivan had taken with Pietro in his office.

She arrived five minutes early for their nine o'clock appointment. Hilary told her to go on into Pietro's office. When she walked in she found Pietro poring over the photographs which he'd spread out atop his big desk. She smiled. He looked so serious. She knew he was under pressure worrying about making a good impression on her father. The success of the campaign would go a long way in achieving that.

She cleared her throat and he looked up at her and grinned. *"Buon giorno."*

"Buon giorno," Ana returned. He looked cosmopolitan in a well-fitting dark gray suit, white shirt and even darker gray tie. His wavy hair fell over his eyes.

He brushed it back with a hand and said, "Ivan did an amazing job on these. Come, have a look."

Ana went to stand next to him and picked up a couple of the photos. "I agree," she said after a few minutes. "What I really like, though, is his emphasis on the contours of the full-figure models, not the ones who're size twelve and under. He truly knows how to bring out the beauty of all body shapes."

They talked for several more minutes about the photos, then chose their favorite shots of each item in the line. When they were done for the day, Ana said, "Have you thought about Ivan any since I brought up the possibility of you two getting together for coffee sometime?"

"Yes," Pietro said, smiling, "I've given it a lot of thought, and I'm interested."

Ana's heartbeat sped up. He'd taken the hook. Now to reel him in, "Good, because I have an idea."

"What sort of an idea?" Pietro asked warily.

"Leave that up to me," said Ana. "Just be at my place on Valentine's Day at 7:00 p.m. I'll do the rest. Won't it be fun, letting someone else plan a romantic date for you and Ivan? All you need to do is look fabulous!"

"I don't know," Pietro began.

Ana interrupted him with, "Don't you trust me?" She cringed inside when she asked him that because what could he say except yes? She felt manipulative.

"Yes, of course, I trust you," said Pietro. She noticed sweat had broken out on his forehead. Why was he so nervous?

"Okay, great," said Ana casually. She picked up

her shoulder bag and began heading for the door, then paused to look back at Pietro. "By the way, my mom told me your mother already knows you're gay."

"You told your mother?" he asked, visibly astonished she would break her promise.

"No, no," Ana assured him. "She told *me*."

"When was this?" he asked, his attention riveted on her.

Ana laughed shortly. "It's funny, really. Mom says your mother doesn't have a heart condition. She suggested somebody was lying. Either you made it up or your mother really told you that when you tried to tell her you're gay. At any rate, according to Mom, your mother is waiting for you to tell her point-blank. She's living in anticipation of that momentous day!"

"Okay, I made it up!" Pietro shouted. "I needed a good excuse as to why I never told her. I've been telling that lie ever since. I'm the one who's not ready. I can't bear seeing the disappointment on her face. She's done everything for me. She worked two jobs to put me through school. I owe her more than making her the proud mother of a gay son. I owe her a wife and children."

Even though Pietro was shouting, Ana calmly said, "She's your mother. All she wants is for you to be happy. Are you happy living a lie?"

"Everybody lives a lie in one way or another," Pietro declared more quietly. "I'm not so different from you, Ana. You were so content with your perfect fiancé. You thought everything was going to be heavenly from now on. Only to have your relationship bomb because he's jealous of the time you spend with me. He's not so perfect after all, is he?"

"Now I get it," Ana said, smiling with sudden enlightenment. "You didn't say anything to Erik because you're jealous of us."

"Give her a prize, she's finally figured it out!" said Pietro, his demeanor not gloating as Ana expected. "I'm a terrible friend. I thought of telling Erik I'm gay that night but then he pissed me off with his attitude. He had you, Ana, and he didn't even have to work for you. You just fell into his arms."

"I didn't just fall into his arms. I tormented the poor man for two years with my neuroses. I was a mess and he stuck by me," Ana said vehemently. Her eyes flashed. "And you have no right to judge him. No right at all. What's more, I'm hurt that you didn't think any better of me that you let your low opinion of Erik keep you from helping me out."

"I know now it should have been about you and me, not you, me, and Erik. Even if Erik loathed me, I should have been in your corner."

"That's what friends do," Ana said.

"I haven't had a close friend since you," Pietro told her, his eyes pleading with her not to give up on him.

"That's nobody's fault but yours," Ana said. "You never answered *any* of my letters."

She grinned and opened her arms to him. He gratefully hugged her close.

"Are we going to beat that dead horse again?" he

joked. Then, more seriously Pietro said, "I'm so sorry, Ana. Please say you'll forgive me."

Ana smiled, "I do," she told him. "Now, I have a favor to ask of you."

"Anything you want," Pietro promised, smiling broadly.

Part one of her plan had worked out quite well. Now for part two.

Abby knocked on Erik's door and hastened inside. She held up a heavy vellum envelope in soft beige. It was hand addressed and included a wax stamp on it with the letter *C* embossed on it. "Look, Erik, it's an invitation from Ana!" she cried, excited for him. He had been a changed man the past three weeks. He was still a kind, thoughtful boss, but he was not as gregarious as he normally was with everyone. When she had first sensed something was the matter and had asked him about it, he'd simply said, "Ana and I aren't seeing eye to eye." Well, that almost broke Abby's heart. She liked Ana, and although she adored her boss it wasn't like her to interfere with his personal life. She was too traditional for that. She could, however, take pleasure in his personal happiness and Ana made him happy.

Erik who'd been going over financial reports stood up and accepted the envelope. Abby wanted to wait and see what was in it, but forced herself to walk smartly from the room.

Erik looked down at the envelope. It was formal. She'd taken such care with it he was sure it held something life-altering. Perhaps something like a note saying she was breaking their engagement. Why hadn't he gone over there as soon as possible as he'd promised his father he would? He knew the answer to that. His manly pride was wounded. For the past three weeks he had been suffering without Ana. Let her suffer a bit longer without him. Then, when he finally came around she would appreciate him more he had foolishly thought.

He broke the wax seal and it crumbled in a red pile onto his desk. Opening the envelope he retrieved the note inside.

You are cordially invited to dinner tomorrow night at 7:00 p.m. at the home of Ana Corelli. The pleasure of your company is highly anticipated. Don't be late. Then, she had simply signed, *Ana.*

With his nerves back to normal, Erik smiled. Okay, she wasn't kicking him to the curb, yet. He still had a chance of winning her back.

He pressed the intercom. Abby answered. "What can I do for you, Erik?"

"Please phone Ana and tell her that her invitation is accepted," he said, his tone decisive.

"Right away!" said Abby.

Somewhere in the city two other men were receiving similar hand-delivered invitations from Ana, although their invitations stated they were invited for drinks, not dinner.

On Valentine's Day Ana prepared an intimate dinner for two. She made sure the wine was chilled well ahead of time. She took special care with her appearance, choosing a short red dress, in honor of the holiday, with strips of material that crisscrossed her back. Her hair fell down her back in soft waves, and the only jewelry she wore was diamond stud earrings and her engagement ring. She glided across the hardwood floor in her favorite pair of black sandals by Jimmy Choo. They were both comfortable and elegant.

Appetizers were put next to the wine on the living room coffee table at exactly seven. She didn't expect anyone to actually show up on time, but her doorbell rang at the appointed hour. She briefly wondered who had shown up first as she walked across the room to get the door.

She laughed softly when she saw that all three of her guests were at her door, every one of them bearing flowers. An 'O' of awe and wonder shaped her red lips and a smile caressed her big brown eyes. "How lucky can a girl get?" She stepped aside, "Three handsome gentlemen on Valentine's Day! Please, come in."

Erik, Pietro and Ivan strode into the loft with smiles on their faces, the epitome of refinement.

They were fakers, all of them. Five minutes earlier, they were at each others' throats of course unbeknownst to Ana. The universe had conspired to have them arrive in the lobby of Ana's building almost simultaneously. Erik walked through the door with Pietro on his heels and shortly afterward, Ivan entered the building and exclaimed, "Erik! I haven't seen you since you and Ana got engaged. Congratulations! How are you?"

Erik who, with Ana, had socialized with Ivan and his partner, Miko, on occasion offered Ivan his hand in greeting. Grinning and sincerely glad to see Ivan, Erik said, "I'm well, and how're you holding up?" Erik had liked Miko, a sushi chef who had owned a small but successful sushi restaurant.

Ivan's long blond hair combed away from his face, smiled wistfully. "Some days are better than others, but I'm slowly trying to get back out there. That's why I'm here. Ana invited me over for drinks. She said she had someone she wanted me to meet."

Erik's expression suddenly lost its friendliness. He glanced at Pietro who had been standing close by because he was an inveterate eavesdropper and he was the only one who had been fully apprised of why Ana had invited all of them there tonight. "I suppose Ana invited you tonight, too?" Erik asked him, his voice cold.

"Brrr," Pietro said tauntingly. "It's suddenly freezing in here. Yes, Erik. My dear, sweet friend, Ana, invited me, as well. Get over it."

Erik was in his face in an instant. "Listen, *Lanza,* I've had about enough of your attitude. Frankly, I don't see why Ana can't see through your smarmy charm. She usually has better taste in friends."

"I thought that, too, until I met you," Pietro returned.

Ivan stepped between them. "Gentlemen, might I interject a bit of logic? It is now three minutes till seven, and Ana said not to be late. I'm going upstairs whether you two follow or not."

The elevator arrived and Ivan stepped into the empty conveyance with Erik on one side of him and Pietro on the other. Not a word was said as the car ascended. On Ana's floor, Ivan stepped off the elevator and walked away, leaving Pietro and Erik to follow. As the two men walked side by side, Pietro said, "I don't know why you dislike me so much. I never did anything to you."

"You didn't deny you want Ana for yourself," Erik accused.

"I didn't say I did, either," Pietro reminded him. "In fact I told you she wasn't my type but you didn't want to hear that."

Ivan had rang the bell already so they picked up their pace. "And I still don't," Erik said, "Because no man who likes women could resist her."

"Say that again," Pietro said pointedly, looking at Erik with a smirk on his face.

Pietro got great satisfaction out of the flummoxed expression on Erik's face. Erik didn't have time to respond, though, because Ana opened the door and the only thing the three men could think to do upon seeing her was smile as if all was well with the world.

Ana hugged Ivan first and admired him in his beautifully cut dark blue suit. The color brought out the blue in his aquamarine eyes. "Thank you for coming. I know it probably wasn't easy for you to let me set you up on, for want of a better expression, a blind date."

Then she hugged Pietro. "I don't think I've ever seen you looking happier."

Pietro wanted to tell her it was due to throwing her fiancé a curveball a minute ago, but held his tongue.

Finally, she turned to Erik and shook his hand. "Good to see you, Mr. Whitaker. It's so kind of you to take time out of your busy schedule to accept my invitation."

She gestured to the couch in front of the coffee table. "Please, sit down."

They did as they were bid and she began filling four wineglasses. "I asked you here to kill two birds with one stone." She handed Erik his glass of wine. "My fiancé believes that something…unseemly is going on between Pietro and me."

"I never said that," Erik began in his defense. "I said I felt you were not telling me something."

Ana ignored him, and handed Pietro a glass of wine. "And my oldest friend has chosen this day to say…"

"I'm gay," Pietro provided the words.

Ivan laughed.

Erik drank his wine in one gulp.

Ana pulled Pietro to his feet and put her arms around him. She whispered in his ear, "You're free now."

There were tears in her eyes. When they rolled down onto her cheeks, Pietro wiped them away. "Good God, woman, I'm the one who's coming out." He set her away from him. "Now, dry your tears and go finish him off."

Ana walked over to Erik and reached for his hand.

He took it and rose with a sigh of resignation. "I've been a damned fool."

"True, so true," Ana said, gazing up at him. "But my dad once told me that men are prone to act like fools on occasion and I should just ignore them when they do, and keep on loving them. Which, I do…love you."

Erik hugged her so tightly, Ana could barely breathe. "So, that's what you weren't telling me."

"It wasn't my secret to tell," she said reasonably. "He had to be ready."

She twisted in Erik's arms to glance back at Pietro and Ivan who were definitely simpatico. They were laughing companionably at something one or the other had said, and from their body language she could tell they didn't mind sharing personal space with each other.

"I should have known that if you weren't completely honest with me you had a very good reason," Erik cajoled, stroking her back.

Ana gazed up at him, "That doesn't make up for the fact that you felt insecure about me," she said, "What's up with that?"

"It's something I'll have to work on every single day we're together," he said honestly. "I'm far from cured. I nearly jumped down his throat a few minutes ago. I regret how I handled the situation. I regret that I hurt you. But I'm not gonna lie and say I'll never have those feelings again. I will promise to react to them in a better manner, though."

"I'll take that promise," Ana told him. She kissed him slowly and deliberately, taking the time to remind him what he'd been missing. When she looked into his eyes afterward she knew that he had gotten her message. He was putty in her hands. However, there was one last detail she had to take care of before their evening could begin.

"Excuse me a moment," she said as she left Erik's close embrace.

"Guys," she said to Pietro and Ivan as she walked over to the foyer table, opened the drawer and withdrew an envelope. Returning to them, she handed Pietro the envelope. "Follow these instructions for the romantic night of your lives. Get going now because your reservation is for eight. That's why I asked that you not be late."

In the envelope were the location of the five-star restaurant where she had reserved them a table and the name of the club they were going dancing at after dinner. "My treat. All you have to do is mention my name," she added with a grin. "Have fun, you two."

She saw them to the door and received grateful kisses on her cheek. "Happy Valentine's Day!" they said in unison.

"Happy Valentine's Day," Ana happily replied.

Erik was standing behind her when she turned around after closing and locking the door. "As for you," she said, pointing an accusing finger at him. "You've been a bad boy." Her eyes were fierce. She poked him in the chest, causing him to back up. "I think you need to be punished."

Erik grinned sexily. "Do with me what you will."

"That's just what I plan to do," Ana told him, as she

grabbed his tie and moved in for the kill. Standing close she slid one long, shapely leg along the inside of his thigh until she reached his package. She felt the pulsating need from that quickly hardening part of him and smiled with satisfaction. "Yes, I think you missed me."

"You have no idea," Erik breathed.

Ana's fingers were busy unbuttoning his pants. He couldn't wait for her to unzip him. He reached down and did it himself. Her hand slipped inside and she rubbed him. He was hard and ready for action.

Erik pulled up her dress and cupped her behind. Ana knew that if she didn't move this to the bedroom soon her neighbors were going to get an eyeful. The big picture window that looked down on the street was stark with no window treatment at all. She kissed him, teasingly bit his lower lip, then took off running for the bedroom. "Work for it," she cried, laughing all the way.

In April, Erik surprised Ana with the rooftop garden he'd promised her. She moved out of her loft into the penthouse, although that bit of information was kept from the families.

Their wedding took place at Erik's parents' home in New Haven in mid June. The garden was in full bloom and the one hundred and twenty guests were pretty loyal about not leaking information to the media about the time and place of the nuptials. However photos of the wedding still found their way onto the internet. Ana and Erik refused to allow any magazine to feature it, though.

On the day of the wedding, Ana was getting dressed

in her bedroom when Drusilla paid her a visit. "Darlin' you're looking a little tired. Is there anything you'd like to tell me?" Drusilla's eyes looked huge behind her Coke bottle glasses and her gaze was relentless.

Smiling at Drusilla's curiosity, "Getting ready for a wedding is exhausting," was all Ana would say. Leave it to Drusilla to intuitively know her secret. She regretted not confiding in Drusilla that she was, indeed, pregnant. However she and Erik had decided that bit of news would be shared with the family at a later date. Her folks were here from Milan and it wouldn't go over well at the wedding if the soon to be father-in-law punched the groom, she thought with a smile.

Ana was not allowing anything to ruin her happiness today. This day in June in New Haven turned out to be picture-perfect: an azure sky, temperature in the lower eighties with just a hint of a cool breeze. Her dress, taken from the Corelli wedding line, was a simple strapless white empire-waist gown with pearl buttons down the back. In spite of Drusilla's pronouncement that she looked a bit tired, she was glowing!

The garden boasted an explosion of fragrant and colorful flowers and plants and the guests were resplendent in their wedding finery, the ladies in intricate hats of various shapes and sizes in all the colors of spring.

Among the guests she spotted her family and Erik's, but also Damon and his partner, Sidney. Pietro and Ivan were there with Pietro's mother, Maria, sitting between them. Leo, Teresa and Julianna Barone smiled warmly at her as she walked down the aisle on her father's arm. And Abby and Harry Sinclair had tears in their eyes.

A baby began crying, which only made her smile all the more. Everyone she loved was here today. Then, she glanced up into Erik's smiling face and her heart knew complete contentment.

When Erik saw her walking down the aisle on her father's arm, his heart was full of joy. He glanced at her belly momentarily, thinking of the life growing beneath her own heart— their child and their future.

Was he nervous on this, the most important day of his life? Not in the least. He'd waited for this day for so long that there was nothing that could spoil his utter pleasure in it finally having arrived.

He felt like the most blessed man on earth.

Soon, they were standing in front of one another and gazing expectantly into each other's eyes. Erik gently took Ana's hand in his.

"Dearly beloved," began the minister in a deep, resonant voice…

* * * * *

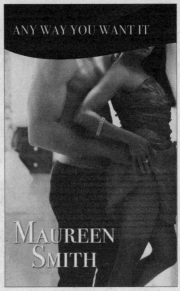

A classic novel in the bestselling Hideaway series!

NATIONAL BESTSELLING AUTHOR

ROCHELLE ALERS

Homecoming

Reporter Dana Nichols has come home to Mississippi determined to uncover the truth behind her parents' long-ago murder-suicide tragedy and finally clear her family name. The last thing she expects is her instant attraction to handsome, dedicated doctor Tyler Cole. As she and Tyler search for answers, they end up walking a dangerous line between trust and uncertainty that will put their future love at stake….

"*Homecoming* is the latest in Ms. Alers' Hideaway series, and boy, what an intense installment it's proven to be!"
— *RT Book Reviews* on *Homecoming*

Available December 2012 wherever books are sold!

REQUEST YOUR FREE BOOKS!

2 FREE NOVELS
PLUS 2 FREE GIFTS!

KIMANI™
ROMANCE

Love's ultimate destination!

YES! Please send me 2 FREE Kimani™ Romance novels and my 2 FREE gifts (gifts are worth about $10). After receiving them, if I don't wish to receive any more books, I can return the shipping statement marked "cancel." If I don't cancel, I will receive 4 brand-new novels every month and be billed just $4.94 per book in the U.S. or $5.49 per book in Canada. That's a saving of at least 21% off the cover price. It's quite a bargain! Shipping and handling is just 50¢ per book in the U.S. and 75¢ per book in Canada.* I understand that accepting the 2 free books and gifts places me under no obligation to buy anything. I can always return a shipment and cancel at any time. Even if I never buy another book, the two free books and gifts are mine to keep forever.

168/368 XDN FEJR

Name	(PLEASE PRINT)	
Address		Apt. #
City	State/Prov.	Zip/Postal Code

Signature (if under 18, a parent or guardian must sign)

Mail to the **Reader Service:**
IN U.S.A.: P.O. Box 1867, Buffalo, NY 14240-1867
IN CANADA: P.O. Box 609, Fort Erie, Ontario L2A 5X3

Not valid for current subscribers to Kimani Romance books.

Want to try two free books from another line?
Call 1-800-873-8635 or visit www.ReaderService.com.

* Terms and prices subject to change without notice. Prices do not include applicable taxes. Sales tax applicable in N.Y. Canadian residents will be charged applicable taxes. Offer not valid in Quebec. This offer is limited to one order per household. All orders subject to credit approval. Credit or debit balances in a customer's account(s) may be offset by any other outstanding balance owed by or to the customer. Please allow 4 to 6 weeks for delivery. Offer available while quantities last.

Your Privacy—The Reader Service is committed to protecting your privacy. Our Privacy Policy is available online at www.ReaderService.com or upon request from the Reader Service.

We make a portion of our mailing list available to reputable third parties that offer products we believe may interest you. If you prefer that we not exchange your name with third parties, or if you wish to clarify or modify your communication preferences, please visit us at www.ReaderService.com/consumerschoice or write to us at Reader Service Preference Service, P.O. Box 9062, Buffalo, NY 14269. Include your complete name and address.

Romantic days…
passionate nights…

Poetry man

Melanie Schuster

After trying everything, including blind dates and online matchmaking, Alexis Sharp has given up on finding Mr. Right. Until hunky stranger Jared Van Buren comes to her rescue. Sexy and sensitive, he is everything she could want in a man. As desire melts their barriers, what will it take to convince the woman who fills his life with passionate poetry that they belong together?

H HARLEQUIN®
™ www.Harlequin.com

Available December 2012
wherever books are sold!

KPMS2851212

Will love be waiting at the finish line?

RACING HEARTS

MICHELLE MONKOU

Dedicated doctor Erin Wilson lives her life cautiously—the opposite of Marc Newton, world-famous race-car driver and her newest patient. But Erin is determined to keep him off the track so he can heal from an injury. Resisting the seductive millionaire playboy's advances takes sheer grit, because Marc is set on racing again…and winning her heart!

"An engaging love story."
—*RT Book Reviews* on *SWEET SURRENDER*